WARRIORS' GATE

It was a mess of a planet, too big and too far out from its sun. If it had ever had an atmosphere, it had lost it long ago. Much of the surface showed long ridges and layers suggesting that water may once have run in the lowlands; sharp-edged wadis cut by storms in desert country, and wide alluvial fans where the storm rivers had hit level ground and dumped their collected silt. Now the water was gone, boiled away millennia before along with the air, and there was only the endless landscape of pale yellow rock.

There was also life. The Antonine Killer was sure of it.

He handled the controls himself, freeing all of the craft's sensors for the ground scan. Command base was over the horizon and temporarily out of contact, otherwise they'd be opening a cell for him right now as his reward for risking a scout ship so close to a planetary surface without the protection of electronic overrides. He stayed low, so low that he seemed to be racing his own shadow as he eased up and over the ridges, and he kept the scan at full power and at its widest angle.

That would have earned more anger from command base, but the Killer knew what he was doing. A wide angle meant a wider energy spread, and he was covering so much ground that a returning signal would be too weak to show. Even a raw cub with his paws on the controls for the first time wouldn't make such a mistake – but then, a cub flew to please his trainers, and a Killer, regardless of what command base might say, flew only to please himself.

He could loop the planet until his motors failed and still only cover an insignificant strip of its surface. Killer intuition told him that the privateer was down there somewhere, hiding in a deeper valley or the long shadow of a mountain, but the chances of fixing it with a scan were small. So he spread the beams as wide as they could go and ignored the feedback on the screens.

When the beam touched, the privateer would know it. The crew would assume they'd been spotted and would try to break away, and their panic would be a flag to the Killer; he'd slide round under them as their engines burned to escape the planet's pull and he'd give them the belly shot, his favourite – a light, carefully placed charge into the vulnerable underside of the privateer, enough to shake the hull with the sounds of a glancing blow or a near miss. The privateer crew would thank their various gods for his bad aim and put their ship into lightspeed before he could circle round for another try – and those grateful prayers would be their last.

That was the beauty of the belly shot, the Killer's speciality. It took out the power of the lightspeed motors and made that final jump spasmodic and self-destructive, a one-way trip to nowhere. It had earned him the respect of the Antonine clan and it kept his record clean with command base – after all, the mandate was for search and capture, not search and destroy.

But, one way or another, a Killer had to be true to his nature.

The sudden breakthrough of radio transmissions warned him that he was no longer screened from command base by the planet's edge.

'Three of their ships gone; we took them out down by the sun. Any sign of the privateer?'

That was the voice of the Control desk. *Three gone.* That meant three clean kills by the Brothers, all of the kills successfully disguised as accidents or self-destructs. He narrowed his scan to within acceptable limits and restored the safety overrides. He heard the voice of the Brother who'd been quartering the massive southern continental plain.

'I had them, and I lost them. They could have gone lightspeed.'

'We'd have seen them go . . .'

It happened so quickly, he almost missed it: a

red-white burn on the line of the horizon, a star that glowed brighter than all the others and which moved against the pattern of the drift.

The Killer was nearest. He rolled the scout ship to follow.

'That's them,' he told Control. 'They're making a run.'

He'd have to be careful, out here within sight of command base. He'd have to seem eager and earnest; so eager, perhaps, that the accuracy of his disabling charges suffered. And then, when the privateer blew a hole in the fabric of space and sucked itself through, he'd have to slap his brow, curse himself for his poor shooting – *damn it, another one vaporised and it's all my fault* – and allow Control to placate him with a few forgiving words.

The acting could be fun, but the killing was best.

Except that he was too far off; his trademark shot needed at least visual identification distance, and the privateer would be at lightspeed before he could get close enough. He increased power so that he was pushed back hard into the scout ship's narrow couch.

The stars outside the cockpit became blurred streaks, but still the Killer knew he wouldn't make it in time. So, it would have to be an instrument shot, or nothing.

The targeting screen compensated for the scout ship's movement and presented a steady view of the horizon and the starfield beyond. The privateer was represented as a moving cross with the numbers of the changing coordinates shown beside it. The Killer's paw moved to the input panel, and he typed in his estimate of the privateer's course. After a moment a second cross appeared, just off-centre from the first. Good, but not good enough; he entered a correction and the crosses lined up exactly, staying aligned as the privateer climbed.

The scout ship's cabin flared white as the charge was fired. All the transparent outer panels were designed to turn opaque for the split-second flash of a launch, but there was always a lag, and the Killer knew to keep his head down and his eyes averted from any reflecting surfaces. When he looked up a moment later, the charge was almost home.

And the crosses were starting to separate.

There was nothing he could do about it now; the energy torpedo was running on its memory towards a spot where it had been told it could expect the privateer to be. An uneven burn from the privateer's motors or an unexpected course change could ruin an instrument shot . . . they had no finesse.

Before the two crosses could split completely, the torpedo hit. Both targets faded, and an overlay on the screen gave the computer's estimate of his success; the privateer had shifted off-centre, but it was an 85 per cent certainty that he'd put one into the engines. Not bad ... almost a belly shot after all.

'Did I bring them down?' he asked Control, thinking, *Do I get to claim the kill?*

'*Main computer says not,*' the controller told him.

'But I got the engines.'

'*Too late. They went lightspeed.*'

It was what he'd wanted to hear. A ship going lightspeed with its engines damaged at the critical moment was taking a long drop with no parachute. Wherever they were heading, they'd never arrive.

Four privateers had tried to run the blockade, all four of them wiped out by the Antonine Killers, the Brotherhood, the clan. The anti-slavery alliance could be fun as long as you didn't take it too seriously.

WARP SYSTEMS HOLDING POWER AT 65 PER CENT
OVERLOAD SYSTEMS PRIMED AND HOLDING
MECHANICAL ESTIMATES – UNAVAILABLE
TARGET ESTIMATES – UNAVAILABLE
SUBLIGHT ORIENTATION – FIGURES UNAVAILABLE
DESTINATION COORDINATES – UNAVAILABLE

FAILSAFE CUT-OUTS DISENGAGED IN ACCORDANCE
WITH SPECIAL EMERGENCY PROCEDURE NUMBER
2461189913 LOG REFERENCE 56/95/54; AUTHORITY
RORVIK, CAPTAIN; SUPPORTING AUTHORITY PACKARD,
FIRST OFFICER

SPECIAL CIRCUMSTANCES QUOTE, EXTRACTED
MINADOS WARP DRIVE GUARANTEE / SERVICE
DOCUMENTS:
'CONGRATULATIONS, BOOBS. YOU'VE SUCCEEDED IN
INVALIDATING YOUR WARP DRIVE WARRANTY.'

The last couple of lines worried Packard more than anything. The privateer's systems failed so often that it was rare for the bridge screens to show a good report, with navigation tools failing most often. But then, most of the time they hardly needed to know where they were or where they were going. That was Biroc's job. Biroc would handle it all.

Packard glanced across at Rorvik. The Captain was across the bridge by the helm, his face showing mild pain at the sound of the emergency klaxons that wouldn't stop roaring until the failsafes were re-engaged. There was no knowing how long that would take; the bump of an apparently inconsequential hit hadn't prepared them for the chaos that began when they moved to light-speed. Every navigation aid had suddenly registered zero, and the inboard computer had panicked and closed itself down – going offline to sort and dump information, it was called, but it was the machine's equivalent of running into a cupboard and pulling the door closed.

Rorvik started to move. He'd said little in the past few minutes, and Packard couldn't tell whether he was being strong and silent or if his mind had simply gone blank. While the crew shouted and argued around him, Rorvik watched Biroc.

And that, of course, was the answer. Take away every navigational aid they had, and Biroc would still get them home.

Packard wondered what kind of damage could take out the stellar compass, the mass comparison probes and the sub-light orientation; take them out in such a way that they didn't simply give wild readings as such units usually did when they failed, but all pumped out a recurring row of zeroes.

It was almost as if they were nowhere. Nowhere at all.

Rorvik moved round the upper gallery of the bridge and leaned across the rail to shout at Packard.

'How bad are the motors?' he yelled, and his voice barely carried over the klaxons' roar.

'We've got damage,' Packard shouted back, knowing that it wasn't much of an answer but having nothing else to offer.

'I know we've got damage, but how bad?'

Packard wanted to shrug but didn't. Rorvik's temper wasn't unpredictable – quite the opposite. It exploded at the least provocation.

It was Sagan, the communications clerk, who came to the rescue. He called across from his own desk. 'Lane's taking a look,' he said.

Lane wasn't the fastest or the brightest of the crew,

but he was the biggest and that counted for a lot. If it was dangerous or dirty, send Lane in; a little flattery kept him happy, and that was cheap enough.

The motor section was isolated from the main body of the privateer by a pressurised double skin, and Lane had to put on a pressure suit and go through a small access airlock in the outer wall of the cargo deck. As the vacuum door slid open, he felt the outward rush of air tugging at him, but after a few seconds that stopped. The sudden silence was a welcome contrast to the sirens that were whining all the way through the rest of the ship.

He moved out to the edge of the gangway and looked down into deep banks of cabling and conduit, the outer layers of the warp motor assemblies. These were lit for remote camera inspection, but the cameras had long been out of use and about half of the lights had failed, putting the motors in shadow. It didn't really matter; the inward-curling rent in the privateer's hull was plain to see and big enough for a man to walk through. Somewhere inside the machinery there was an irregular flashing. That could easily become a fire in the presence of atmosphere.

Look and report, that's what Lane had been told, and that's all he intended to do. There would be no extra praise if he climbed down to the lower catwalks for a closer view, and none at all if he managed to get himself sucked out of the hole in the privateer's side. He went over to the communication point by the hatch and plugged in a lead from his suit.

'Lane to the bridge.'

Sagan heard him and patched his voice through the bridge loudspeakers for Rorvik's benefit. It was Packard who answered.

'What's the news?' he said, aware that Rorvik was moving in behind him.

'Not good. The skin's holed, and there's damage in the warp.'

Rorvik leaned over, practically elbowing Packard aside to get to the microphone. 'How long will she run?'

'She's burning out. If we don't get back into normal space-time right away, forget it.'

Rorvik turned and shouted across to the helm, 'Hit the brakes! Normal space now!'

The helmsman was Nestor, and he started to shake his head. He couldn't attempt to jump back into normal space without some kind of target, but the instruments were useless and Biroc wasn't giving him anything.

'We're drifting,' he said. 'It would be a blind shot.'

Rorvik quickly moved away from Packard and down to the navigator's position. The alien lay half-reclined on a seat of riveted bare metal, strapped down and gagged by a breathing mask; even his head was locked into place by a clamp. Only his right hand had a degree of movement, and this was severely limited by a manacle linked to a heavy chain. He could reach his input panel, and that was all. Rorvik crouched and leaned in close so that only Biroc would hear.

'Hear me, Biroc,' he whispered harshly, 'and ride those time winds right. Because if you don't, I'll have you punished.'

There was no way for Biroc to respond, but his eyes fixed on Rorvik and their expression was murderous. As Rorvik moved away, Biroc tried to watch him. But the clamp held the leonine head rigid.

Biroc was a Tharil, a time-sensitive, one of the most valued navigators on the spaceways. That value was shown not in the wealth or the respect that he could command, but in the price that his abilities would bring on the open market. He was easily worth two or three times the cost of a raw young Tharil snatched from his village and smuggled out past the Antonine blockade, experienced as Biroc was and with a proven record of accuracy.

Time-sensitivity was the Tharils' curse; from an infinite range of possible futures they could select one and visualise it in detail as if it had already come to pass. Sometimes in moments of extreme trance their bodies would shimmer and glow, dancing between those possible futures and only loosely anchored in the present. It took intense concentration to bring a Tharil back into phase with the moment.

Or chains. The heaviest chains would do the job just as efficiently.

Biroc was aware that Rorvik had moved to another part of the bridge; he clearly had full confidence that the Tharil would obey, and wouldn't need to be watched. Biroc had resisted once. He'd expected to be hurt or even killed, thinking that either would be better than the chains, but Rorvik had responded with a better idea. He'd called for the youngest of the Tharils to be brought up from the slave hold. Young Tharils were the least valuable, as time-sensitivity only became controllable with adulthood. Rorvik had then killed the child in front of Biroc and called for another.

The memory made Biroc want to roar and to fight, as always. But there was no fighting. There were only the chains.

He closed his eyes and started to visualise.

The more probable futures always came most easily: a limited range of destinations, the ship arriving safely – he only needed to read off coordinates and feed them into the input panel by his manacled right hand, and the vision would become reality. More remote probabilities were harder to see and impossible to realise, but dreams of freedom and escape were Biroc's only recreation during the long hours in chains.

Biroc frowned. The picture wasn't shaping up as it usually did. There was a green swirling fog that pushed its way before him, a view of space that was unfamiliar

14

and almost emptied of stars; deep within it an object was turning, tumbling top over tail. He concentrated, tried to bring it closer. It was an artefact of some kind, blue and with the proportions of a double cube.

Biroc reached out, pulling the chain taut. He made a fist, flexed his clawed fingers, and started to set coordinates.

Adric hadn't been travelling with the Doctor and Romana for long, but he knew enough to stay out of the way during a crisis. He sat over by the wall alongside K-9, knees drawn up under his chin, a silent observer of the action.

'I think I'm ready,' Romana was saying as she checked the last of the settings on the TARDIS console. Adric could see that she was tired and frustrated, and barely concealing it. The Doctor was standing with his hands thrust deep into his pockets, gazing at the screen which showed the TARDIS's outside environment. The view of E-Space showed little more than a green-yellow fog.

'Try it with the couplers back in this time,' he suggested, without looking over.

'Same coordinates?'

'Yes, why not?'

He sounded agreeable enough, but hardly interested; happy to let Romana handle the haphazard, stabbing jumps that were getting them no closer to escaping from this pocket of a substratum universe that they'd somehow wandered into. It was as if he knew that any course of action was likely to be as effective or ineffective as any other – luck alone would have to bail them out, and no amount of close attention or urging could influence luck.

Romana plugged in a couple of U-links that had been removed from the console and then reached for the switch to activate the settings.

Adric leaned slightly towards the mobile computer beside him and whispered, 'Don't they know where they want to be?'

'Knowledge is a resource, achievement an end,' K-9 piped without any regard for discretion, and Adric was left to think about this for a moment as the TARDIS's lighting dimmed in response to the new energy routings.

Romana was giving the screen a doubtful glance. 'This isn't going to work,' she said as the image faded, indicating that the TARDIS was in transit.

'How can you say that,' the Doctor argued, 'when you don't even ...' The screen image re-formed, the familiar green swirl. 'No, it isn't going to work. Try it again.' He walked round to watch Romana as she re-patched the U-links.

'Admit it,' Romana said. 'You don't know what you're doing.'

'I don't know what I'm doing.'

'You're just being random.'

'I'm following intuition. That's something else.'

'Intuition won't guide us to the CVE. A signal from Gallifrey might.'

'Oh, no,' the Doctor said, moving away again as if to escape the argument. 'Let's not bring Gallifrey into this.'

Their need to find the CVE wasn't in question; the CVE was the invisible and undetectable two-way door that had first dropped them into E-Space. Relocate it, and they could find their way out.

But looking for a signal from Gallifrey, like a beacon for an errant child who couldn't even find its way home ... The Doctor seemed surprised that Romana had even suggested it. Even Adric had noticed how she'd avoided the subject of Gallifrey ever since their summons to return. The one time he'd asked her about her home planet, she'd all but shut him down.

But now she said, 'At least admit the possibility. They may know we're here and be trying to help.'

'I don't need any help from Gallifrey.'

'It's better than tossing a coin.'

The Doctor was about to answer when an idea seemed to occur to him. 'Why is it?' he said.

'What?'

'What's so improbable about tossing a coin?'

Adric had seen this ploy from the Doctor before. It came about when his argumentative reserves were running low, so he'd turn the tables and take over his opponent's ideas leaving them nothing to fight with. Romana gave a weary sigh. Adric knew how she felt. Watching it being done to someone else could be fun; having it done to you, and not for the first time, was only tiresome.

Romana gathered the spare U-links and moved off towards the door connecting to the rest of the TARDIS.

The Doctor followed, getting well into his theme. 'Didn't you ever hear of the I Ching?' he said. 'Random samplings to reflect the broad flow of the material universe?'

'I'm not impressed,' Romana's voice came back faintly.

The Doctor glanced across at Adric and K-9, and flashed them the smile that meant mischief whatever the circumstances.

'Don't go away,' he said, and vanished through the door.

The privateer was getting a thorough shaking. Rorvik had to hang on to the rail by the helm to keep from being pitched over to the lower gangway levels. He shouted at Nestor, 'It doesn't matter where, just get us down!'

'Don't yell at *me*,' Nestor protested, and lifted his hands to show that the controls were moving without any help. 'Ask Biroc what he's playing at!'

The shaking ended as suddenly as it had begun, and the sirens began to wind down. Crewmen started to blink as lighting levels were restored from red-wash to normality. Only a couple of low-level beeps and hoots continued, signals of minor damage resulting from the rough handling. That was normal for any flight.

Rorvik said, 'Is that it? Are we stable?'

Somebody sighed, somebody giggled, one or two crewmen started to flick switches on the desks before them.

Rorvik tried again. This time there was a hint of menace in his voice. 'Maybe you thought it was a rhetorical question. I had the mistaken idea there was a crew somewhere around here to give me answers.'

Packard quickly cut in from the technical systems point. 'The motors are shut down, we're not travelling. Other than that, I can't tell.'

'Can't tell?'

'The instruments.' He gestured at the panels in front of him. 'Shot.'

Biroc lay in his restraints, exhausted and drained. His eyes were rolled upwards and half-closed. Rorvik said as he moved towards him, 'I hope you played this right, Biroc. Because if you didn't . . .'

He was wasting his time. Biroc was deaf to all threats.

Rorvik gestured across the bridge to Sagan. 'Take him below and patch him up.'

19

Sagan hurried forward, touching another crewman on the shoulder as he came round the walkway. The crewman, whose name was Jos, got up and joined him without arguing; nobody wanted to risk Rorvik's annoyance, not right now. They went either side of the navigator's chair and started to unchain the Tharil.

Rorvik, meanwhile, made his way across to the technical systems point. 'Well?' he asked Packard, who looked down at his display screen.

Packard said, 'According to this, we never made it back into normal space-time.'

'Meaning?'

'We're stuck somewhere that isn't even supposed to exist.'

'If you don't understand the readouts, say so.'

'I don't understand the readouts,' Packard admitted readily, and Rorvik turned to Nestor. Sagan and Jos had by now freed Biroc, and they were taking an arm each to drag his inert form towards the bridge stairway and the lower decks. The alien was giving them no help.

'Report from the helm,' Rorvik demanded crisply.

Nestor looked around, uneasy.

Rorvik added, 'That's you, remember?'

'What do you want me to say?'

Rorvik closed his eyes, wearily.

The corridors that ran deep into the storage and service areas of the privateer were as run-down and disreputable as the rest of the ship. One of her crews, many years and several changes of owner before, had decorated the passages with spray paint so that the walls now showed a continuous rolling landscape of crudely drawn flowers and plants hovered over by huge bees and butterflies. Maybe the scenes had been intended to be cheerful, but down here, with the noise and the permanently stale air and the darkness, it was like a long-haul bad dream.

Biroc was far more aware than he was letting on. Sagan and Jos were starting to tire under his weight and, now that they were away from Rorvik and had nobody to impress, they slowed down. There was a sign that read *Cargo/Main Locks Access*, but it had been painted over and a crude arrow drawn in underneath it – another relic, this time of some old remodelling. They paused here for a moment to get their breath but started to move again before Biroc could stir; neither would want to see him awake before he could be secured.

They slowed again after a few yards. Biroc was keeping himself as limp as before and his dead weight was wearing them down; he was sliding away from them now, and they could barely support him.

'Hold on,' Sagan said, and they stopped to get a better grip, pulling Biroc's arms across their shoulders and around their necks for maximum lift.

Biroc came upright suddenly, using them to get his

balance. They were still staggering in surprise as his powerful arms clamped tight around their necks, making them squawk and choke at the same time.

There was no chance of their being heard, and as long as Biroc kept his grip there wasn't much chance of their reaching the weapons on their belts, either. Jos threshed around the most and Biroc gave a squeeze to discourage him, and as the alien's attention was diverted for a moment Sagan managed to get enough room to reach for his sidearm.

It never cleared its holster. Biroc took three paces towards the nearest door and threw them both forward. Two heads made the door ring like a dinner gong, and the crewmen slid to the floor with limited interest in what was going on around them. Biroc didn't see them land; already he was running.

He could feel himself starting to shimmer out of phase, but he got a grip. Right now, he needed total concentration on the present, but the shimmering was a good sign – it meant that his achievable futures were multiplying as a consequence of his action.

He'd never been alone in the below-decks area of the privateer before and he didn't know which way to go. But he was a Tharil, a time-sensitive who could direct ships across galaxies; surely he could steer himself from the inside of one rusty old crate to the outside. He paused at an intersection, looked around and, following strong instinct, chose a direction.

The slave holds were below him, he could feel it. Hundreds, maybe even thousands, of his own people, stacked like cards in a deck and drugged into placid sleep by the slave ship's life-support systems. These were feed tubes and pumps that barely sustained existence, in conditions that otherwise would kill more than half their number.

The call to go down to them was strong, but Biroc had to resist. The tenuous outline of a future that he'd seen under the chains had set him on a different course. The vision of it would guide him in when to act and when to hold back, but it didn't offer him any special protection. Other, less successful futures could easily prevail.

No alarms were ringing yet, but it could only be a matter of minutes. He rounded a corner and then, at a sound, pulled back; he dodged into a doorway to conceal himself as a panel slid open somewhere ahead. There was light beyond the panel, and the long shadow of someone moving in the light.

Lane stepped from the access lock into the main corridor. He cracked the seal on his helmet and removed it with relief. His nose had been itching for more than five minutes and he'd nearly dislocated his neck trying to rub it against the inside of the visor. Finally, he treated it to a good scrub from the rough fabric of his glove.

Otherwise he might have seen Biroc coming. But he didn't and was barged aside as the Tharil ran to beat the sliding door.

Lane stared ahead for a moment, slow to react because he couldn't quite believe what he'd seen. If he hadn't known better, he'd have said that a Tharil had just pushed past him to get to the warp chamber. He turned to take a second look and saw the lock panel closing.

It was crazy. Tharils didn't run loose around the ship, and if one did, why would he want to trap himself in a sealed-off engine compartment? One with no hatch to the outside?

Except that the damaged compartment had something just as good as a hatch – a man-sized opening ripped by an Antonine torpedo.

Lane ran to the door, but the warning lights had already changed; the second door was open and so this inner door was sealed. He reached instead for the intercom point by the frame.

'Lane to the bridge,' he shouted. 'Emergency!'

Biroc was shimmering as he looked down from the catwalk to the damage below. Cabling continued to spark. There was a crackling sound, and a brief show of flames before automatic extinguisher jets damped it down. Flames betrayed the presence of atmosphere.

Like a prisoner following a breeze through a

dungeon, Biroc looked for its source. He saw a white fog blowing in through the hole in the privateer's side, and beyond it a light so bright that it was almost painful. Biroc started to descend, allowing his attachment to the moment to loosen as he moved; the shimmering increased and he became almost transparent, letting himself stretch out to test a range of possible futures before he committed to any.

As he came nearer he could sense it: the sweet air of his people just beyond the jagged hole – the time winds.

Like it or not, Romana was being drawn into the Doctor's argument. Adric stood in the doorway of the TARDIS control room and watched; Romana was on her knees and sorting through a small box filled with odds and ends of junk, searching for a match to the U-link that she had in her hand. The Doctor wasn't interfering, almost as if he really did think that the solution to their problem might be something other than technical.

'How about astrology?' he was saying, and Romana was shaking her head.

'Better things to do with my time,' she said.

The Doctor tried another angle. 'What do you think is the biggest common factor in the belief system of every developed culture?'

'Based on your example of astrology? Ignorance.'

'No, faith.'

'Same thing.'

'The belief that the universe is actually going somewhere. Every race watches the stars and sees them moving in patterns. They see how every universe moves in an even mathematical progression and they look for some guiding principle that they can apply to their own existence.'

'You can't predict the courses of people the way you predict planetary movements.' Romana turned her back to Adric for a moment and, when she turned again, she had another box to sort through. Anybody who wanted to observe an intuitive arrangement in contrast with a logical index would only have to look at the Doctor's storage system; most of the stuff in this box didn't even belong anywhere in the TARDIS. 'You just can't,' she went on. 'There are too many random factors that shape behaviour.'

'Only because the number of factors affecting a life is too vast to calculate,' Doctor said. 'But if you could construct a formula which relates those factors to the greater flow of cause and effect ...'

'You'd have a formula as big as the universe, and as difficult to handle.'

In spite of Romana's dismissal, Adric was beginning to think that he could understand what the Doctor was saying. Put a thousand grains of sand in a jar, and no matter how random their order the final position of each would be determined by the courses and actions of all the others The number of possible futures open to each grain would be so immense that, as Romana had said, any attempt to chart them mathematically would be impractical. But take a few of the grains at random, and from them extrapolate a pattern ...

Adric wasn't sure whether the idea was a piece of unscientific fancy, or a glimpse into a system on another level to any conventional scientific approach.

'But think of E-Space,' the Doctor was saying. 'A universe of very little matter, all spread thin. Simplified relationships between bodies means a simpler formula to explain them – and a random act like the fall of a coin begins to gain significance.'

The toss of a coin? Could that be it: a question asked, a coin tossed into the air, the answer implied in its fall – the coin being that one grain of sand in whose behaviour one might see a subtle reflection of the greater pattern?

Adric dug around in his pocket and came up with a golden token. A Decider had given it to him when he was seven years old, an early reward for those of academic promise. It wasn't real gold; the coating was molecule-thin, applied by a technology that had been lost long before the Decider was even born. But as a substitute for a coin it would do nicely.

One flip didn't seem like much to hang a choice on. A series of flips would be better, he thought, giving randomness a chance to average out and the true pattern to show through; but a pattern would then imply a more complex interpretation than a simple yes or no, and there wasn't the time for test flips to establish an idea of what those interpretations ought to be.

Romana, meanwhile, was plainly irritated. It showed in the way that she stirred the boxed components about, as if she'd lost track of what she was looking for. She said, 'It's mumbo-jumbo and superstition. It won't get us anywhere.'

'It's an idea,' the Doctor said.

'Hardly.'

He knelt by her, and gently placed his hand over the box to stop the search. 'Anyone would think you didn't want to go back to Gallifrey.'

She looked at him suddenly, as if he'd whipped the cover off a secret that she'd been concealing even from herself. But whatever she was going to say, admission or denial, had to be put aside as the TARDIS started to move.

The Doctor reached the control room first, Romana only just behind him. The control column on the TARDIS's operational desk was rising and falling. Adric stood beside it feeling pleased with himself, but this satisfaction was undermined when he saw the Doctor's expression.

'What did you do?' the Doctor demanded. He

looked around for K-9 and saw the mobile computer unmoved from its place by the wall.

Adric backed off a little. 'Random numbers in a reduced universe, Doctor,' he said.

'Never mind that, what did you *do?*'

'I tossed a coin.'

Even as Adric spoke, Romana was looking over the console settings. She was almost amused; they couldn't be in any greater danger than before, as the TARDIS could be trusted to keep them safe in transit whatever the coordinate settings were. The Doctor's pique more probably came from his being faced with a hard test of one of his less substantial fantasies.

She said, 'Are you saying you didn't want to be taken seriously?'

Ignoring her, the Doctor advanced on K-9. 'You saw all this?' he said.

'Affirmative, master,' K-9 replied promptly.

'Well, why didn't you warn me?'

'It was in accordance with the theory you were offering, master.'

Romana added, 'If you're not prepared to back up one of your theories with a simple experiment . . .'

She was interrupted as the TARDIS lurched violently; her thought as she grabbed the console edge was, *This isn't possible.* But loose objects were falling and there was an ominous rumbling like the first signs of an earthquake. Adric was out of sight and the Doctor was down, and K-9 was *sliding* . . . she realised that the floor was tilting, that the timeless, no-space inaccessible zone of the TARDIS interior had suddenly become accessible to an attack.

The Doctor was yelling at her; even so, she could barely hear him over the noise. 'I don't know where we've landed,' he was shouting, 'but get us out!'

She realised that he was too far from the console to see the readouts. He'd leapt to the conclusion that they'd materialised in some unsafe environment.

'We haven't landed anywhere,' she called back. He couldn't make it out, so she added, 'We're still moving.'

'That's impossible,' he said, and Romana thought, *I know that.*

The Doctor flinched as the wooden hatstand hit the wall with a crash and then started to bounce around downslope. Lights were flashing that had never been needed before, and alarms that had sounded only in tests were now sounding for real. The Doctor rolled over; K-9 was between him and the entranceway, the robot's underside traction wheels squealing as it tried to stay in place on the canted floor. Beyond K-9 there was a slit of light, the significance of which didn't reach the Doctor for a moment; he wasn't slow to understand, but it took an effort to believe.

The even, regular forces that normally held the

TARDIS in shape were starting to bend. The outer door was opening onto ... nowhere.

The slit widened, and a white fog started to blow in under pressure. It was backlit brightly and moved by forces the Doctor had never believed he'd see: the time winds. Adric was emerging from below the console, barely balanced on hands and knees, his head shaking groggily as if he'd banged it. The widening beam lay on the floor like a slice, and Adric was crawling towards it.

The Doctor shouted a warning, but it was unheard. He reached Adric and pulled him back just as the full brilliance of the light hit the console. Romana crouched in the console's shadow as glass covers popped and exploded and the panelling started to burn.

The bright edge continued to travel. K-9 was still struggling, and it had almost reached him. The Doctor reached to pull the robot to safety, but it was too far; the light struck, and the mobile computer started to take the full force of the time winds. That same light fell upon the Doctor's arm; he gasped and fell back, quickly thrusting his hand into his coat.

The doors were wide open, and the time winds ran through K-9 like desert sands. They poured through his joints and seams, ageing and altering as they went; the robot's outer casing became dull and scarred, and there was no way of telling what changes were taking place inside – not that the Doctor could watch for long, because his attention had become fixed on the maelstrom to which the TARDIS had been opened.

It was a void, and they were being tipped towards it – emptied out as a curious giant might shake strange objects from a bag. The Doctor made sure of his grip on Adric's collar with his free hand, and glanced towards the console and Romana. She was protected for the moment as long as she didn't try to move out, and as long as the console wasn't stripped away by the energies lashing at it. K-9 had weakened and was sliding back faster, but he was now out of line with the doors and was in no danger of tumbling out. Their safety here was relative – if they were to fall into the void then the time winds would quickly take them apart – but the protection of the violated TARDIS couldn't last for long.

Adric was trying to shout something, but the shaking and the roaring were now so loud that the Doctor couldn't hear him even at a distance of only a couple of feet. But he could see the disbelieving expression on the boy's face, and when he followed his eyes the Doctor saw why.

Out in the void, somebody was running.

Too far away to make out yet, it was definitely a figure in roughly human shape. It moved slowly and with great effort, but still it moved through the hostile zone that was outside of time and space, ploughing on against the time winds and with the opened TARDIS as its obvious destination.

It fought its way nearer, showing itself to be taller and stronger than a man, and finally crossed the edge of the void and entered the control room. Once through the inner doors, the stranger turned and took a hold on them; his face towards the battering now, he started to put his strength into closing up the TARDIS. The strain was tremendous, as if he were singlehandedly closing the gates of Troy, and the shimmering aura that could now be seen to surround him began to flicker and seem unstable.

The stranger was tall and broad-shouldered, basically human in form although his features were like those of a lion; his hands were broad paws, and what showed of his face, head and chest was covered with a tawny-gold fur that was swept back in a mane. His ears were high and pointed, his mouth wide with the tiny points of fangs showing. He wore a baggy white swash-buckler's shirt that was torn and stained in a couple of places – he might have been on the run from a fairy tale.

The doors were closed and, with the time winds excluded, the alien's aura pulsed as he climbed the sloping floor towards the console. Even though the more immediate danger had been suppressed, still the TARDIS shook with the hammering of the void.

Romana scrambled aside as the alien surveyed the controls, flexing a claw ready to operate. The Doctor released his grip on Adric's collar and the boy half-walked, half-slid down the floor to where K-9 had lodged, dust-caked and still, against the wall by the door. As the Doctor moved towards the desk the robot tried to speak, but it came out as an unintelligible slur.

At the console, the Doctor watched as the alien set coordinates. Even when slowed and distorted by the shimmering, its hand moved with an assurance that suggested it had performed such operations before.

'We've got to stop him,' Romana said, but the Doctor put a restraining hand on her arm.

'Don't touch him,' he warned.

'But ...'

'Watch his hand.'

They watched as it drifted across the console. The coordinate keys sank and lighted only moments after it had moved on.

'He isn't fully on our timeline,' the Doctor said, sounding pretty certain even though he could only be guessing.

Romana wasn't buying it. 'He should be torn apart!' she protested.

The alien rotated the lever that would put the coordinates into effect, and almost immediately the rumblings that shook the TARDIS were underpinned by a more even vibration. The stranger sank exhausted to his knees and rested his forehead on the console.

One by one, the alarms were dying down.

'What is he?' Romana breathed, as if she was afraid the alien might hear. 'What did he do?'

The Doctor had no ready answer, other than to state the obvious. 'I think we've just been hijacked,' he said.

'But he came from *outside* the TARDIS.'

The stranger raised his tawny head. He looked at them for the first time.

'Can he see us?' Romana whispered. The aura blurred his image considerably.

'Probably the same way that we see him,' the Doctor said and then, as the alien blinked a couple of times, went on, 'Nice of you to drop in, but if you'd given us more warning we could have tidied the place up a bit.'

'What are you?' Romana added, and the Doctor gave her a sharp look.

'What are you? Is that the kind of contact etiquette they're teaching on Gallifrey these days?' He stopped abruptly, because the alien was trying to speak.

The sound was slurred, and seemed to come from a long distance away. The first attempt was a meaningless roar, but he tried again.

'*Biroc regrets the use of your craft . . . but others follow.*'

'Others?' said the Doctor. 'What others?'

Biroc carried on, as if he had an urgent message and only a little time to deliver it. '*Believe nothing they say. Not Biroc's kind.*'

'Look, you can't simply . . .'

The TARDIS lurched again, and the floor dropped

35

almost level. The Doctor and Romana fell back at the shaking, and as they came up again Biroc was moving and the door was opening under its own power.

Adric watched the awesome figure pass as it loped sluggishly out into the void. The last of the alarms cut out and left them with silence.

The silence was complete. No time winds blew, no forces worked to warp the TARDIS and hold it open; it was like any normal landfall.

The Doctor moved towards the door. Romana was about to call a warning, but she checked herself as she realised that the dangers, however they had originated, were no longer present.

While his back was to the control room, the Doctor carefully withdrew his hand from his coat and wrapped the end of his scarf around it. There was almost no feeling, but he didn't look; it was as if he knew what he would see – or was afraid of it. Instead, he turned his gaze to the landscape outside.

There was nothing in any direction, nothing at all. Just an even, burned-in white, a complete blankness that was hard to look at. He took a step back into the TARDIS.

'That was Biroc,' he said, somewhat unnecessarily.

'I know,' Romana said as she came around the control desk to look at the alien's settings.

'Any idea where he brought us?'

'I don't know. The coordinates are all locked off at zero.'

'A line of nothings,' the Doctor said. 'That's exactly what this place looks like.'

WARP SYSTEMS TO 40 PER CENT AND FALLING
CHECK HULL FOR POSSIBLE BREACHES AT 01/00/5768 – 5775
SELECTIVE ELECTRICAL SYSTEMS FAILURES – REFER PROGRAMME 01/00/2375 FOR SPECIFICS
LEAKING SPIGOT IN REC ROOM COFFEE DISPENSER

WARNING: INFORMATION ON PRESENT LOCATION COORDINATES REMAINS UNAVAILABLE.
WHAT ARE YOU PLAYING AT, GUYS?

Packard cleared the screen of its standard readout – nobody ever paid it much attention anyway – and keyed in the code for a display of new sensor information. A single bright dot appeared and rapidly sketched in the double cube that was the privateer's perception of the TARDIS. Then, with a little flourish, it rotated the skeletal image through three dimensions.

'What do you call that?' Rorvik demanded.

'Some kind of alien artefact,' Packard said. 'Could even be a ship. It's what Biroc headed for as soon as he was out.' Packard was tempted to add, *And there's nothing else out there*, but he didn't.

Rorvik turned away from the screen and moved to the gallery rail. The bridge structure was set around a central well, a pit that was open all the way down to the lower decks and the maintenance areas. He sighed heavily. Maybe the privateer's control deck had once been gleaming and efficient, but that had been a long time ago. Now it was badly lit and filthy, the theme colour being that of rust. Any paint was streaked and aged, fixtures were held in place with tape, glass covers to screens were split and cracked. Beyond the helmsman's position a line had been rigged, and a greasy old set of one-piece underwear was hanging to dry. The garment looked unsalvageable, all holed and patched.

The crew were lounging and sprawling around, doing nothing in particular, content to let Rorvik do all the worrying for them. Sagan and Lane were playing cards, Jos was flipping screwed-up pieces of paper at a waste bin and mostly missing, and Nestor had taped a torch to the gooseneck stalk of his talk-back microphone. Under its light, he was giving himself a manicure with an ornate dagger.

But for once they were all at their posts, which was something of an upside. Rorvik said to Packard, 'You got us into this. Start thinking of a way to get us out.'

'It wasn't me who decided to run the Antonine blockade.'

'I didn't hear you argue. Now we've got a busted warp motor and no navigator – nowhere to go and no way of getting there.'

Packard indicated the video. 'I say we should try to contact that ship.'

'For what?'

'They might have somebody who can fix a warp motor.'

'Would they be stuck here if they did?'

'We won't know until we find out.'

'And we'll still need Biroc back. Or we'll have to wake up one of the slaves in storage.' Rorvik raised his voice to make it carry to everybody on the bridge. 'And even if the slave survives – which is doubtful – it cuts into the profit on the run. That's a chunk out of everybody's bonus. You want to complain, bring it to Mr Sagan here ...' (Sagan looked up at the sound of his name) '... because he's the one who managed to lose your navigator for you.'

Somebody booed, somebody else blew a raspberry.

Rorvik turned to Lane. 'We're going out to that ship,' he said, pointing to the screen where the outlined shape still revolved. 'You'll be leading the way.'

'Why?'

'In case they're hostile. Who would you rather see shot? Your captain, or you?'

Avoiding the question for some reason, Lane said,. 'How will I find this ship in nothing but mist?'

'Portable mass detector,' Packard cut in. 'Get it from stores.'

'Meet in the cargo dock,' Rorvik added, and then, for Packard's benefit, 'We'd better go dig out the sauce-pans and beads.'

It was council of war in the TARDIS. The Doctor, Romana and Adric were all hunkered down around K-9. Romana touched the robot's side gingerly; it was pitted like a relic.

She said, 'Is this caused by the time winds?'

The Doctor nodded. 'Poor old thing wasn't built to take this kind of treatment. He's charging, but . . .'

Adric said, 'You can repair him, can't you?' He sounded anxious.

The Doctor considered a kindly lie, but decided against it. 'No, Adric, I can't.' He showed him a couple of small wafers. 'These are a part of his memory.' Under a slight pressure, one of the wafers crumbled and disintegrated.

'Memory wafers are replaceable,' Romana objected.

'If you've got replacements.'

Adric glanced forlornly towards the storerooms. 'And haven't you got any?'

'I've used all those I've got. They're not nearly enough.'

'It's ridiculous,' Romana said. 'One of the commonest components around; you can buy them in buckets on Gallifrey.'

'K-9 won't make it to Gallifrey,' the Doctor said quietly.

Romana stood up. She became suddenly businesslike. 'And nor will we if we don't apply ourselves to the problem.'

The Doctor rose a little more slowly, wiping his good hand on his scarf. 'Well,' he said, 'we're not in E-Space. But then we're not in our own universe, either. I think we must be between realities, caught in the moment of translation.'

'Hanging in the gap.'

'Right.'

'And somewhere else . . .'

'Somewhere else in nowhere,' the Doctor corrected her. 'Somewhere else in nowhere, the doorway we've been looking for has to pass through, hasn't it?'

Romana nodded. 'But because it's nowhere, we'd never find it.'

Adric offered helpfully, 'I could try tossing the coin if you like . . .'

He was saved from murder by the sudden return to activity of K-9. All attention turned to the robot.

The Doctor said, 'How are you feeling, K-9?'

'Basic misconception of the functional nature of this unit,' K-9 chirped, sounding healthier than he looked.

'Unit neither feels nor finds it necessary to express states of efficiency or dysfunction.'

'Does that mean you feel all right?'

A short hesitation, and then; 'Decidedly not, master.'

'How much control have you got? Have you checked through your systems?'

'There is nothing wrong with this unit's systems. Concern yourself with the three men who are approaching.'

The Doctor shook his head sorrowfully. 'This is not good. He's having delusions.'

But Adric was looking at the screen. 'Doctor, look!' he said, and two heads swung in response.

Where the screen had previously shown a white expanse of nothing, there were now three silhouettes. Their outlines were firming up as they approached through the mist, and they seemed to be wearing some kind of uniform; the figure in the lead carried a bulky apparatus that sat on his shoulder and extended a probe ahead. He seemed to be concentrating on a small readout before him. As they watched he paused, and made a small correction in angle that brought the party square-on to the TARDIS.

'That's three impossible things,' the Doctor mused. 'Must be time for breakfast.'

'What?' Romana said, mystified.

The Doctor looked thoughtfully for a moment at

the complete memory wafer that was still in his hand. Then he stowed it in a pocket. 'Never mind. I'm going out – wait here, and don't show yourselves.'

Lane was having a problem with the figures that the mass detector was giving him. He shook his head and tried making another minor correction, but then Packard's hand was on his shoulder. Lane frowned and looked up, and Packard pointed. The blue double-cube, or ship, or whatever it was, stood only a few yards ahead. Behind them, Rorvik was trying to smooth some of the creases out of his uniform and look like a captain.

A door opened in the front of the box, and a man stepped out.

He wore a long burgundy overcoat that wouldn't have been out of place on a pre-technology coachman, and several yards of scarf that went a couple of times around his neck and then took a few turns around his hand, which was stuffed halfway into a pocket.

'Hello,' the stranger said. 'Call me the Doctor. Always nice to get a visit from the neighbours.'

Rorvik hadn't expected to be met – at least, not by somebody of a normal human size. Even if this man stood alone in his box, he'd barely have room to turn round. Putting his prepared speech aside, he said, 'I'm Rorvik, this is Packard, and the beast of burden over there –' he indicated Lane – 'is just one of the crew. I know this sounds like a stupid question, but have you seen our navigator?'

'It depends,' the Doctor said, and he seemed quite eager to be helpful. 'What did he look like?'

Packard cut in. 'He looks like a Thark with a Thoat's head.'

'Really? Well, it would be hard to miss somebody as distinctive as that, wouldn't it?'

'His name's Biroc and we're pretty worried about him. He's a Tharil,' Rorvik added with a knowing wink. 'You know what they can be like.'

'Left you stuck in the void, has he?'

'Too right,' Packard said with obvious annoyance. 'Dropped his chains and scooted. It was all we could do to—' Most of the breath was driven out of him as Rorvik's elbow thumped firmly into his ribs. 'To follow,' he finished hoarsely.

'This Biroc,' the Doctor said. 'The Thark . . .'

'With the Thoat's head.'

'With the Thoat's head, he wouldn't by any chance be, well, loosely anchored on the timeline, would he?'

'You *have* seen him!' Rorvik said, although Packard thought that he was overdoing the surprise.

'He hijacked me and brought me here, and then he ran off into the void.'

'Really?' Rorvik said excitedly. 'Which way?'

The Doctor looked around into the uniform blankness, and shrugged.

Rorvik's excitement died as he realised what the Doctor was saying. Packard, meanwhile, had his eyes on Lane; the crewman had moved a small distance away from the group and was studying his mass detector readings. He seemed puzzled.

Rorvik said, 'That's the trouble with Tharils. They're so temperamental. Sometimes they just get triggered off and go into a big depression. Get all kinds of complexes – Biroc started imagining he was being kept a prisoner on his own ship. Can you imagine that?'

'Ridiculous,' Packard agreed, although most of his attention was still on Lane.

Rorvik said, 'Did he happen to mention anything about . . .'

'Being kept a prisoner on his own ship?' The Doctor shook his head. 'Not a thing.'

Packard had moved over to Lane, and was studying the readout over his shoulder. Now both men looked confused, but Packard half-nodded to himself.

'Well, that's a relief,' Rorvik said. 'I mean, it's promising, considering his condition and everything.'

'Very.'

'I'm sorry, I didn't catch your name.'

'Everybody just calls me the Doctor.'

Packard was now moving away from Lane. His eyes held a message for Rorvik as he spoke, a sense of urgency. 'Perhaps the Doctor would like to join forces with us,' he said.

If the Doctor had caught that glance, he didn't show it. 'I doubt that there's much I could do for you – you're so well-equipped.'

He indicated the mass detector. Lane was banging it with his fist.

'True,' Rorvik said. 'But then, we could hardly leave you here, could we? And I feel kind of responsible for what's happened.'

'This isn't the place to make plans,' Packard said. 'Why don't we all go back to the ship?'

The Doctor paused for a moment, while Rorvik and Packard worked to convey innocence and concern. They were like two alligators smiling at a lamb.

The Doctor said, 'Give me two minutes to lock up,' and stepped back into the TARDIS. The door closed behind him.

Rorvik turned to Packard. 'What's bothering you?' he demanded.

'I don't know, but let's string this Doctor along.' Packard had the feeling that there was a message in the mass detector's anomalous readouts, if only he could decipher it. 'We can't tell what he may be able to do for us.'

Inside the TARDIS, the Doctor was explaining pretty much the same idea. 'We can't tell what I may be able to get my hands on,' he was saying. 'If they've got a mass detector, they may have compatible memory wafers.'

'Why not just ask them?' Romana said. She'd

observed the scene on the exterior viewer, but she hadn't been able to catch much of the undercurrent of distrust.

'Believe them, you mean? Remember what Biroc said.'

'Why believe Biroc?'

'He was running, wasn't he?' And, seeming to consider that this was sufficient explanation, the Doctor turned to go back outside.

Travelling in the void was an unnerving experience. There were no reference points at all, and without the mass detector it would have been impossible. The detector had originally been designed for freighter crews to check on cargoes without having to enter the holds; they simply ran the probe along the walls and got a reading of the mass concentrations beyond it. Now it served equally well as a navigation aid, although Lane was wondering if it was safe to trust it – how reliable could you consider an instrument to be when it indicated that an object was larger on the inside than on the outside?

Lane stayed ahead with his eyes on the instrumentation, and the others lagged behind with their eyes on him. Everybody needed something in sight to give them horizon, or else the featureless white around them would start to spin. And yet, the void wasn't total; there was a sense of up and down, and they were breathing. Even if zero coordinates truly meant nowhere, at least there seemed to be a faint leaking-through of reality from somebody's universe. Find the source, and perhaps you'd find the exit.

The mists swirled and parted, and the Doctor caught sight of the dim, bulky outline of Rorvik's ship for the first time. Although the details were indistinct and hazy through the fog, he could see the nose towering high above them at an angle over a wide base; it was like looking up at a giant frog about to spring.

'This is it?' the Doctor said.

Considering the circumstances, it was a pointless question, but Rorvik didn't seem to mind. 'That's her,' he said proudly.

'Does she have a name?'

'Used to have. The paint came off.'

'What is she? Passenger transport?'

Rorvik was about to answer, but then he seemed to change his mind. He finally said, 'Freighter. Low-bulk and high-value cargoes.'

It seemed to the Doctor that they went a longer way round than was necessary to reach the entrance to the loading bay, but he said nothing.

They climbed a shallow ramp to enter. The bay was a fair-sized, greasy utilitarian chamber, with exposed struts that supported the curved outer wall and an open-mesh floor under which cabling could be seen.

Packard was the last in, and he stopped by an intercom. 'Party aboard,' he said. 'Make safe the hatchway.'

'What?' came an uncomprehending voice from the other end of the line.

'Close the door on the hold,' Packard said wearily.

The ramp withdrew into the ship, and the outer door lowered – a huge and ominous shutter. The Doctor watched it; he wasn't exactly apprehensive, but when a door like that closed there was no mistaking that you were being shut in. Somewhere behind, Lane was struggling out of the mass detector rig. The shadow of the door fell as a hard edge across them all.

'This way, please, Doctor,' Rorvik said pleasantly.

Leaving Lane behind, they walked through an archway and out of the bay.

On the bridge some distance above the entering party, Nestor was still at his post and still working on his nails. Over by the entrance doors, Sagan, robbed of his partner and tired of playing solitaire, was trying to build a house of cards and had reached the third level. Jos and another member of the crew were by the navigator's position with its chains and restraints. They were holding up an undersized tarpaulin between them and inspecting it critically.

'It'll never cover it,' Jos said. No matter which way they tried to arrange the sheet, some part of the restraints always showed.

Up on the helmsman's board, an indicator lit up with a shrill beep.

'Watch out,' Nestor said. 'They're here.'

The two crewmen hurriedly threw the tarpaulin to cover the chains as best they could, as the door slid open and Rorvik strode through

'And this is the bridge, Doctor,' Rorvik said. 'Nerve centre of the whole operation.' With a casual side-flip of his hand, he demolished Sagan's house of cards and continued the motion into a sweeping gesture that included the whole area. He looked back to see his guest's reaction. The Doctor walked on past, looking around, trying to seem impressed.

Observing his apparent interest, Rorvik went on, 'My team. Best drilled you can get, efficient as anything on the spaceways. Isn't that right, lads?'

There was a general grunt from around the bridge. It could have meant anything and certainly wasn't the rousing cheer that Rorvik had summoned, but he let it pass. 'Nothing these boys can't do when they put their minds to it.'

'Except spring us from the void.' The Doctor was lifting a corner of the tarpaulin and looking underneath. 'Why the chains?'

Jos and his fellow-crewman exchanged a nervous glance. Rorvik came round to take a look, and his eyes widened as if he'd never seen them before. 'Chains?' he said. 'What chains are those?'

The Doctor lifted the tarpaulin a little further to show. 'The ones with the shackles.'

'Ah!' said Rorvik, as if suddenly remembering. 'Yes. Those chains.' He turned to Packard. 'What were they for?'

'Biroc asked for them,' Packard said, improvising.

Rorvik forgot his growing embarrassment for the moment. He was interested to see what excuse Packard would come up with. 'Really?' he said. 'Why?'

'For when it gets rough.'

Rorvik nodded as if he'd just been told something new. He turned back to the Doctor, but the Doctor had gone. He bobbed back up into view by the helm, on the highest level of the bridge.

Nestor stared as the Doctor looked over his shoulder at the control panel.

'Don't let me disturb you,' the Doctor said. 'Just carry on.' But Nestor continued to stare, boots up on the console and manicure forgotten. 'I do believe,' the Doctor continued after a moment, 'that this is a standard Minados panel, isn't it?' No response. 'Yes, I thought so. May I just ...' He reached across the helmsman's boots and touched a button. Along with the rest of the crew, Rorvik turned in surprise as a large screen illuminated and threw light across the whole bridge.

'How did you do that?' Packard said with suspicion.

Rorvik moved forward for a closer look, all else forgotten in a moment of wonder. 'I never even knew that worked,' he said.

The Doctor began to descend to the main bridge

level. 'That's your exterior viewer. You mean to say that you've always managed without one?'

'Never needed it. Biroc did it all.'

Up at the console, Nestor was still staring at the buttons that the Doctor had touched. He reached out and prodded one experimentally, like a chimpanzee with a piece of unfamiliar fruit.

'Well,' the Doctor said, 'now you've got something new to play with.'

The image on the screen frame-rolled a couple of times as Nestor dialled around different cameras mounted on the ship's exterior. Each view showed the mists of the void, with only some part of the ship in the foreground to distinguish it from the angle that had gone before.

All the crew were transfixed by the images. And because the screen was now the centre of attention, Rorvik crossed over and planted himself in front of it.

'Now listen, Doctor,' he said. 'You seem to know your way around a piece of space machinery, and I'm going to make you a proposition. I don't know how you get on in that little ship of yours, but I bet it isn't very comfortable. I'm going to offer you a free ride with us, if you'll just join in with our plan to . . .'

He stopped. Everybody was turned his way, but they were looking through him as if he didn't exist.

'Nobody's listening to me,' he said with a frown and a dangerous hint of petulance.

Packard stepped forward with a warning shake of his head, and indicated the screen with a glance. Rorvik turned.

One view was held on the screen, and as he looked it became a little clearer with image-intensifier circuits coming into operation.

The enhanced picture showed a gateway, two massive wooden doors set in an arch of mason-cut rock. Two decayed pillars supported a partly collapsed lintel; there was a ruined statue to one side, an empty plinth with a heap of rubble around it on the other. The stone was white and grey, and it blended off into the mist. One of the doors was slightly ajar.

'What is that?' Rorvik said.

Packard looked towards the Doctor, as if to say, *You found it, you tell him.*

The Doctor considered for a moment. Then he said, 'At a guess, I'd say that's where your navigator was headed.'

Biroc stood in the gloom of the hall, and looked upon the lost glory of the Tharils. He knew that he was in the midst of a legend, but it was a legend of defeat – no more than an echo of the greatness that had preceded the enslavement of the race, the fall which had scattered them throughout a thousand systems to live as land-grubbing beggars while they waited for the hunters to drop from the sky.

All around him lay evidence of the final struggle. At

his feet, a long-dead Tharil, no more than fur dried onto a skeleton, pinned under the decapitated shell of a robot warrior. The head lay where it had rolled some distance away, a skull-mask grinning through the protective mesh of the battle helmet. Wires, relays and a snapped central strut showed in the open neck. The robot was coated with dust but otherwise seemed barely touched by the ages, while the Tharils' decay was almost complete.

That had never been the way in the days of the Greatness, the days when the Tharils ruled all of time. By what tragedy had they failed to foresee their own defeat? Biroc stepped over the two bodies and moved through an archway.

The door was beyond. It was a perfect mirror; no dust had ever touched its surface or ever would. Biroc regarded his reflection – a pitiful state for one of a race of kings . . . but no matter.

The warriors' gate would belong to the Tharils again.

The Doctor joined the privateer party as they set out towards the gateway; as before, Lane led the way with the mass detector. This time the party was bigger, and not much effort was made to conceal from the Doctor the fact that it was heavily armed. Nobody tried to stop him coming along – after all, he was more or less responsible for the discovery of the gateway – but he could tell that Rorvik was now keeping a wary eye on him.

The mass detector brought them within sight of the TARDIS again.

They were going to pass it at some distance, but the Doctor suddenly said, 'Since we're here, can you just hang on for a moment?' And he was off before he could give Rorvik a chance to think of a reply.

Romana was trying to carry out some additional repairs on the weather-beaten K-9. She wasn't getting very far. The main problem seemed to be that he couldn't hold much of a charge; he'd soak up as much power as could be pumped into him, but as soon as the connections were broken his energy levels would start to dwindle. It was like emptying water down a deep hole.

'What's the capability estimate now?' she asked as she reconnected the charging cable to a wall socket.

K-9 hesitated for a moment as he made the internal survey. Before the time winds, the response would have been instantaneous. 'Sixty-five per cent.'

'It can't be that low. Not already.'

'This unit guarantees accuracy within the limits of the data available. No refunds are offered on the grounds of displeasure.'

'What?'

'Query imprecise. Additional data required.'

Adric had moved in to stand behind Romana, and was looking over her shoulder. 'He's dying, isn't he?' he said quietly.

'Robots don't die,' Romana said. 'They aren't alive.' But she knew she didn't really believe it.

They both looked up as the Doctor entered. K-9 started a slow spin to face him.

The Doctor waved aside their questions and said, 'I want you both to stay out of sight – they still think I'm alone. How's K-9?'

'Getting worse,' Romana said. 'Did you get hold of any memory wafers?'

'There wasn't much chance to look, and I don't think I trust them enough to ask. Now we're all trailing off to look at some ruin in the void.'

Romana looked at him. 'What should I do?'

The Doctor was almost at the door. He didn't want to give Rorvik time to add more suspicions to his scrapbook of dark thoughts. 'Try to keep the old boy in one piece until I get back. There are some static charge blocks lying around somewhere – you could try rigging those in sequence to take some of the strain off the memory.'

He didn't stay long enough to say goodbye.

Rorvik was trying to communicate with the privateer by hand radio, but reception was poor. He finally got through and spoke to Packard, who had stayed behind as acting commander so that, in Rorvik's words, they, quote, *wouldn't invite another disaster by leaving this bunch of louts unsupervised.*

Rorvik said, 'Anything from the analysis yet?'

Another of the reasons why Packard had stayed behind had been to take over Sagan's duties while the communications clerk worked on a computer breakdown of the puzzling results of the mass analysis of the Doctor's craft. 'Nothing yet,' he said. 'Sagan messed the figures up and we had to feed them in again.'

'All I want is a straight answer. Is he worth squeezing for information, or not?'

'No way of knowing.' Which was as straight an answer as Packard could manage.

By now, the Doctor could be seen heading back towards the party.

'Thanks a lot,' Rorvik said. 'Wind it up, he's coming back.'

Packard flicked a couple of wrong switches before he managed to close the radio channel. He hadn't much experience on the communications desk. From the nearby computer input panel, Sagan muttered, 'You didn't have to blame it all on me.'

Packard leaned back, stretched, and locked his fingers behind his head. 'Why not? It was all your fault.'

Sagan half-turned in his seat. 'Why are we playing around with this Doctor? If he knows warp mechanics, he can help us. If he doesn't, he can't.'

'Got to be careful,' Packard said. 'We don't know which of his buttons to push yet. He could be an honest man.'

Their eyes met, and then they both looked away, shaking their heads. Honest men – a species beyond understanding.

Romana watched the exploration group on the TARDIS's screen, following them until there was nothing left to see. Then she turned to Adric.

'Come on,' she said. 'Work to do.' She led the way towards the storeroom, saying, 'Any idea what a static charge block looks like?'

'Er . . . no,' Adric said as he followed her through the doorway.

K-9 was alone, apparently inert. But his systems came to life without any warning.

'Unit functional and awaiting orders,' he piped. 'Unit functional, master.' It was a pale shadow of his normal speaking level; there was no one in the room to hear it, and it didn't have the volume to carry any further.

'Master?' K-9 queried, and turned his head for a weak scan of the control room. 'Unit is functional, master . . . requesting instructions . . .'

There was a pause of more than a minute, during which the robot's operational signal lights flickered and almost failed.

But then he said, 'Assuming typical memory lapse on the part of the Doctor. Responsibility lies with the unit to pursue and correct.' And with that he lurched forward, only to be snapped to a halt as the connecting power cable came taut.

He rolled back a little and tried again; the plug snapped free, and the cable trailed behind as he circled round to the door. As he approached, K-9 extended an antenna; there was a brief pattern of electronic notes, and the door swung open.

K-9 rolled forward, out into the void in search of his master.

As the Doctor had seen from the privateer's bridge, one of the gateway's heavy doors was slightly open. There was darkness beyond it. He studied the faces of his companions: every one of this party of half a dozen intrepid souls looked to be trying to think of some little hesitation which wouldn't be obvious but which would slow them for long enough to be the last across the threshold.

The result was that the entire group came to a sudden halt, coughing, sneezing, an unexpected grain of dust in the eye.

Except for the Doctor, who turned by the open door and said, 'What's the matter? Not deserted enough for you?'

Rorvik seemed to realise that he set no example by hanging back. Starting forward, he indicated the door and said, 'What makes you think Biroc made for this place?'

'Because apart from both our pieces of transport, this is the only other location in this non-universe that has any substantial reality. There was literally nowhere else for him to go. Come on.'

The door swung all the way open. There had been no breeze, and the Doctor hadn't touched it; he hesitated, but almost immediately recovered his brightness – or, at least, some of it. He stepped through, and the others moved to follow.

It took a moment for even the Doctor's eyes to adjust to the vaulted stone tunnel. It was so much gloomier than the void outside; there were the remains of elaborate mounts for burning torches along the walls, but these were now empty and broken and skinned over with cobwebs. The paved floor was dusty and marked by a single line of tracks – Biroc's.

The Doctor led the way now as the group followed the tracks down along the tunnel and into the banqueting hall, to a scene frozen in time and aged a thousand years.

There was an open fireplace filled with dead ashes. Over the mantel a square of torn canvas sagged, black and mildewed, from a gilded picture frame. Windows to either side were so stained and filthy that no light could get in, and the heavy velvet drapes were almost eaten away.

The Doctor wondered, if the glass could be cleared, what landscape those windows would look onto.

Somebody gasped. As the immediate impression of decay began to settle out into individual details, evidence that they were standing in the middle of a scene of battle became apparent. Those fallen, twisted shapes on the floor that so resembled stacks of old burlap were in fact the bodies of the slain, and the traditional-looking sets of armour that were ranged around the hall were not empty suits but something far more sinister, aged into immobility.

Their pattern was not random; there was one to each archway, and beyond each warrior was a perfect mirror.

As nothing moved and no obvious threat was offered, the group began to spread throughout the hall. Its main feature was a large banqueting table down the centre; the table had once been set for a meal which had been left to rot. There were piles of mould where the fruit bowls stood, bones with shreds of black meat still clinging. The candelabra were cobwebbed, and most of the chairs had been thrown back or overturned.

Only Lane was still by the entrance tunnel, where with a thankful sigh he was unloading himself of the weight of the mass detector. Rorvik stood in the middle of the room and looked around. At the far end, wooden stairs led up to a minstrels' gallery and the suggestion of an even greater maze of passages beyond; one of the crewmen was climbing.

'What makes you think you'll need that?' the

Doctor said, and Rorvik looked down with genuine surprise at the gun in his hand.

'Didn't even know I'd pulled it. Must be this place.'

'You can see that nobody's set foot in here for years.'

'Except Biroc.'

'Yes,' the Doctor agreed, 'except Biroc.'

Rorvik was drawn away by a shout from another of the crewmen who'd moved to explore a side-alcove. For a moment the Doctor was alone and unobserved, and he took the opportunity to pull his injured hand from his pocket and loosen the folds of scarf around it.

He winced at the glimpse he got: this was now the hand of an old man, wrinkled and scarred. And he couldn't be sure, but he thought that the damage had spread a little. His arm was starting to ache.

He followed Rorvik to the alcove. It was a small, white-plastered chamber off the main room, perhaps once a small chapel or storeroom.

There he saw the cause of the excitement; Biroc's footprints were across the floor. They disappeared at an arched doorway that was completely filled by a mirror.

Rorvik stepped forward, his free hand out-stretched. His fingers touched their own reflection; the mirror was hard and unresisting, and his touch left no mark.

A force field of some kind, the Doctor supposed; it repelled all matter and deflected all energy, including light.

'He's here somewhere,' Rorvik said. 'I want him found.'

Ferreting through some of the many darker corners of the TARDIS, Romana discovered four static charge blocks buried under a heap of newspaper reports on the battle of Waterloo. The newspapers were fairly fresh. This was more than could be said of the blocks, which looked as if they'd been salvaged from some ancient device fit only to be scrapped.

Romana presented the static charge blocks to Adric. Each block was a lightweight cube of foam with two simple connections: power in, power out. Romana explained that they could be linked to work in sympathy with any memory circuit, but that they could neither replace it nor work on their own. The electrical bonds that held the molecules of the foam together could be altered by fairly low applications of energy, and could be patterned to hold information; a small piece of the block could then reproduce the information in its entirety. No specific part of the block held any particular piece of information. It all lay in the pattern. Any cut or surge in the power supply tended to wipe or distort the pattern, which gave the blocks a limited practicality.

And these blocks weren't new, and they weren't the best.

'I don't even know if they'll take the current,' Romana admitted as she and Adric moved through into the control room. 'But all we can do is—'

She stopped as she saw that K-9 was missing. The socket was uncovered and empty, and the door was open to the void.

'Oh, no,' she said.

'Where did he go?' Adric said.

'Good question. Take these.' Romana handed the four blocks to him and headed for the door.

Adric called after her, 'What are you doing?'

'I'll have to get K-9 back before he wanders off too far. Don't leave the TARDIS.' And with that, Romana left the TARDIS.

Once outside, she looked around into the void for the first time; the impact of its total whiteout was far greater than it seemed within the safe frame of the viewing screen. She took a few steps and felt a rising panic, but it vanished when she turned and looked back at the TARDIS, her only stable reference point in an otherwise empty universe. She wouldn't go so far that she lost sight of it; that could be fatal.

As she turned away again she thought she caught a sound. She held her breath and listened; very faint and very distant, but it was unmistakeably K-9.

Orders, master? Orders?

She couldn't be completely certain of the direction, but she thought she had a good idea – and if she hesitated, K-9 might move too far away.

She set out to follow.

*

Where the banqueting hall was gloomy, the cellars beneath it were dark as pitch. The Doctor carried one of the candelabra from the main table, and it threw long shadows down the spiral steps as he descended.

The stairway brought him to a paved vault, apparently some kind of weapons store; it was difficult to make out any details as the candle flames danced, but there were some simple pikes and spears in racks the full length of one wall, and what looked like Tharil body armour on wooden stands. The attack on the gateway, whenever it had happened, must have been a complete surprise; none of the weapons had been moved.

The armoury, like every other room in the place that he'd seen, had a mirrored archway with an immobile warrior planted before it. Another warrior, badly damaged, was slumped against the wall near the stairs; it had probably staggered down, sparking and twitching, to run headlong into the stonework.

In the candlelight, the undamaged mechanical warrior in the archway looked even more sinister. Its design was plain, a hard outer shell with overlapping plates to protect joints and a double-mesh before the sensor rig in the head. It was this arrangement that gave the effect of a caged skull. The warriors up above had carried different weapons. This one carried an axe.

Not all of the tackle in the armoury was so easy to

identify. The Doctor set the candelabrum down by a heap of silver globes and picked one of them off the top. As he raised it, the dust sifted away from the surface leaving it clean and mirror-bright.

The shadows danced and the Doctor turned. Had a slight breeze fanned the flames, or had someone moved in the room behind him?

But there was nobody, only the one damaged warrior and the other one stilled by time. He turned his attention back to the globe.

It was too large and too heavy to hold comfortably. A creature bigger and stronger than a man would find it fit for hefting and throwing. One of Biroc's size would find it ideal.

But what was its purpose? The material, if it could be called a material, was similar in nature to that of the archway mirrors. Dust and grime didn't cling, and its reflectiveness was total.

As was demonstrated when the Doctor saw the robot warrior with its axe raised behind him.

In the fisheye distortion of the globe, the axe began to fall.

The Doctor dodged, almost too late; he felt the passing wind of the blade tug at his sleeve as it sliced through the air.

Time didn't seem to have blunted it much, although the jarring ring of metal on stone as the axe tried to bury itself in the floor sounded like bad news for the edge. The warrior seemed to be locked in place for a moment, and the Doctor scrambled back; the robot's responses were lagging by a second or so as it came about and started to follow.

'Now, now, old chap,' the Doctor said, looking for a reaction and seeing none.

Come on, the Doctor told himself, this is the armoury. Something around him had to be useful. And if the sagging figure over by the wall was anything to go by, these warriors could be damaged and even destroyed

Well, there was one weapon that was literally to hand. It took all of his strength, but he threw the globe.

The warrior saw it coming and lifted the axe, swinging it like a bat. The flat of the blade caught the globe and smashed it aside, squarely into the chest of its damaged fellow. There was a bang and a bright flash; the globe vanished, and the damaged warrior was immediately covered with a layer of frost. Its hands came up in a brief spasm of animation, and it slid the remaining distance to the floor.

As it hit the ground it broke up, aged to fragility in an instant. The globe was an actual time bomb.

The live warrior, meanwhile, was still advancing, and its reactions seemed to be improving. The Doctor took a step to the side, and the warrior began to circle. It was as if the Doctor's act of resistance had taught it caution; it was looking for an opportunity to move in, but didn't want to leave itself open to attack. Not that it was in any danger – the Doctor was weaponless, one-handed and, by comparison, frail.

But at least one of those conditions could be changed; circle a little more, and the Doctor would be within reach of the rack of pikes.

'You know,' he said quietly, 'it's obvious you're only a machine. Anything with half a brain would know it could just wade in and finish me off.'

Perhaps that was a mistake; something in the way the warrior turned its head seemed to indicate that it had begun to understand, though the invitation wasn't being taken.

Nevertheless, it bought the Doctor a little more time. He reached the pikes and grabbed one, swinging it around in front of him.

The axe flashed up and down, and there was a jarring that nearly popped his shoulder out of its socket. He staggered back a couple of paces; the pike had been reduced to a four-foot length of wood with a splintered end.

He was almost backed up to the mirror, pinned down within the framing arch. There were noises and shadows in the stairway at the far end of the cellar; Rorvik's men must have heard the explosion of the silver globe and were coming to see what had happened.

The warrior heard the noises, too. As Rorvik and Lane came round the spiral, it moved in for the kill.

The Doctor slammed the shortened pike between the warrior's feet and gave a hard twist. The warrior pitched forward, wildly unbalanced, and threw out a three-fingered hand to stop itself against the mirror.

It carried on through.

The mirror swallowed the robot, seamlessly and without a trace.

'What are you playing at?' Rorvik demanded as he crossed the paved floor.

'Thanks for your concern.' The Doctor indicated the mirror. 'Have you ever seen this material before?'

'There's one over the sink in my cabin.'

'Not like this . . . the warrior could pass through, but we can't.'

Lane was over by the wall, looking down at the damaged robot. 'Biroc could,' he said.

At that point there was an urgent-sounding call from Nestor, up in the main hall, and the Doctor pushed further speculation on the properties of the mirrors aside as he moved back towards the stairs.

It was hardly surprising that Rorvik's men should be concerned; they were bunched in a tight semicircle, every one with a weapon drawn, and every weapon shook nervously. An exotic creature had rolled in from the void without any warning, and even now was menacing them.

'K-9!' the Doctor said with delight and shouldered his way through the defensive ring.

'Master?' K-9 said, and he sounded stronger than before. 'Unit functional and requesting . . . requesting . . .'

'Instructions,' the Doctor urged.

'Requesting instructions.'

'Is that yours?' Rorvik said, and the crewmen started looking at one another uneasily.

'He certainly is,' the Doctor told him, and then he stopped to study the instrumentation on the robot's upper panel. 'K-9,' he said, 'give me your efficiency rating.'

'Efficiency rated at seventy-two per cent.'

'Better than it was . . .' He looked up at Rorvik. 'Can your men sort me out a reasonably complete specimen of those robot warriors?'

'Why?'

'So we can find out why there's a thousand-year-old battlefield in the middle of the void.'

Rorvik nodded to Lane, who moved out and summoned a couple of the other crewmen.

As Rorvik's men were discovering that the warriors were heavier than they appeared, Adric was wandering through the TARDIS. He'd been instructed to remain. But there was little to see that he hadn't seen before, and he was bored.

At the control desk he stopped and ran his hand idly along the edge; as he looked at the re-patched

U-links that represented Romana's efforts to get them out of E-Space, an idea started to form.

The door to the outside was still open. Adric stepped out and looked around into the void; the golden coin, the token that had caused all the trouble, was in his hand.

You have to ask a question, he thought – probably at least two questions for a navigational fix.

Gold sparkled against white as he spun the coin to choose his direction.

Meanwhile, over at the gateway, Rorvik's men had dragged a complete warrior over to sit, head slumped forward, by the fireplace in the banqueting hall.

The Doctor had removed the armoured panel of its chest to expose the inner workings, and had spent a few minutes making tests and noises, alternately of satisfaction and disappointment. Now he'd run several lines from the warrior to K-9, and was putting final touches to the linkup. Rorvik and Lane watched over his shoulder.

'What will that do?' Rorvik wanted to know.

'Stick around and watch,' the Doctor suggested. 'Power up, K-9, but take it gently.'

There was a hum as the mobile computer diverted power into the warrior. A few small lights began to glow deep in the chest, but nothing more seemed to be happening. The Doctor turned to speak to Rorvik.

'Of course,' he said, 'there's no way of telling how long—'

Suddenly and without warning, the warrior's head snapped erect and it made a stiff attempt to rise, yelling in an unearthly rasping voice.

'*Exterminate the brutes!*' it barked, and the Doctor called to K-9.

'No, K-9!' he shouted. 'Memory circuits only!'

The warrior's cry ended in a strangled gurgle, and it subsided to the floor.

'This had better be good,' Lane muttered. He re-holstered the pistol that he'd drawn as he'd skipped back.

The warrior seemed safe enough now. The Doctor moved in closer.

'Who are you?' he said.

'We are Gundan. We exist to kill.'

'To kill what?'

'*Kill! Kill the brutes! Kill them all!*'

'Details and background to programming.'

The direct technical command seemed to calm the warrior. 'Specify.'

'Who made you, and why?'

'The slaves made the Gundan. The slaves, to kill the brutes who rule.'

The word slaves caused a glance to pass between Rorvik and Lane.

The Doctor didn't miss it. He said, 'Tell me what happened here.'

'The Gundan were sent where no slaves could go; we faced the time winds and we lived. We came upon the masters without warning – no guards, no strength, and only their Gateway to flee for safety.'

'A gateway? Where?'

'Here is their Gateway. Here is their tomb.'

'The mirrors – they lead to other places, other times?'

'A Gundan to every mirror. No brute could pass, no brute could live. And so the slaves became the masters.'

'And the slaves were . . . ?' the Doctor encouraged.

'Men. Men the slaves and Tharils the masters, but nevermore. After the Gundan, the brutes go in chains for eternity.'

So I've seen, the Doctor thought, but he only said, 'Power down, K-9.'

He half-turned away from the Gundan as he began to rise.

The warrior quickly reached out and seized his arm, but its grip soon weakened and began to slide away.

The Doctor shook himself free.

Rorvik was forcing a smile. 'Quite a story,' he said. 'You think any of it's true?'

'Well,' the Doctor said carefully, 'what does it matter? It was all a long time ago. The important thing is that this could be the gateway which will get us all home.'

It was certainly important. But it seemed that there

were also other issues which, once understood, would not allow themselves to be ignored.

It was unlikely that Packard, if he'd climbed to the helm and dialled around the camera positions which showed various angles on the void, would have been able to see Romana in any of them; and for her part Romana couldn't see the privateer, or the TARDIS, or the gateway, or anything at all. The deceptive nearness of K-9's calling had lured her out further than she'd intended to go, and when she'd lost the sound, she'd lost her only remaining orientation.

If Packard was going to watch anybody, he was going to watch Sagan.

Sagan's discomfort made him laugh. The communications clerk was still transferring figures from a small roll of printout to the main computer keyboard; this was his fourth attempt.

'It's not my fault,' Sagan protested. 'Who did these figures?'

'Lane did them. They're the results of the scan he did on the Doctor's craft.'

'I know that.'

'Very good!' Packard said approvingly.

'They don't add up.'

'You're not supposed to be adding them up.'

'I mean, if you believe this, the thing's bigger inside than it is outside.'

'Are you holding that sheet upside-down?'

'You're talking,' Sagan said stiffly, 'to a professional.'

'Paid idiot,' Packard corrected. 'I'll call Rorvik.'

As Rorvik moved away to take the call, Lane was running the probe of the mass detector over the mirror to which Biroc's tracks had led.

'Anything?' the Doctor asked him.

'Just a reflected signal from this room. It shouldn't even be possible, but that's what I'm getting.'

It was then that Rorvik called Lane over, and they stood where they couldn't be overheard. Rorvik seemed quite friendly. Lane was immediately suspicious.

'Just been speaking to Packard,' he said. 'Sagan's having trouble with your figures.'

'I only gave them as I read them.'

'Yes, but you know what Sagan's like. Go back to the ship and straighten him out.'

'What's the problem?'

Rorvik glanced across the hall. 'The Doctor's the problem. Or maybe he's the answer to one.'

'I'll need this,' Lane said, indicating the mass detector. Without it, he'd have no way of locating their ship in the void.

'There's another one coming.' Knowing the way that his men's thoughts would soon be turning, Rorvik had ordered Packard to send a man across with lunch.

Lane shrugged, and moved towards the entrance

tunnel. On the way, he passed by K-9. The mobile computer had been disconnected from the Gundan.

Lane didn't hear the tiny pop of an implosion or see the flash that accompanied it in the panel on K-9's back; nor did he notice the mobile computer swing round and follow him out.

Nobody else saw it, either.

Rorvik was watching the Doctor, who stood before the mirror; the Doctor tapped it with his foot, as if it were a bicycle tyre.

No effect.

Rorvik believed that the mysteries of the Gateway, like most problems, could be solved by a sufficient application of brute force. One simply had to work out where or on whom to apply it.

Biroc was gone. Rorvik was resigned to the risk and expense of reviving another Tharil and chaining him to the navigator's chair. That still left the problem of the warp engine. But the Doctor was here, and every new development showed him to be more capable and resourceful than Rorvik had suspected.

A useful ally. Or, should he be found unwilling, brute force usually made a cooperative prisoner.

On the privateer's bridge, Sagan was still one-finger typing.

Packard said, 'Lane's on his way to help you with that.'

'I don't need help,' Sagan said, somewhat offended.

'Leave it and get down below. Rorvik wants you to go along to the slave hold and get one of the Tharils. See if you can revive it.'

'I'll need help for that.'

'Take whoever you need. Take Aldo and Waldo.'

'Thanks a lot,' Sagan said.

Aldo and Waldo roamed around the privateer emptying the litter bins. Rumour had it that they were passed on to Rorvik along with the ship, but he wasn't warned about the arrangement until it was too late.

Sagan pushed himself away from the input terminal. Revival was a harrowing job, and he'd welcome help from anyone.

Anyone other than Aldo and Waldo.

As Sagan was explaining to crewman Dulles how lucky he was to be chosen to assist, Lane was worrying over another apparent malfunction in the mass detector. It was giving him a reading for the privateer, so he wasn't exactly lost, but there was something wrong with the reading itself: by his reckoning the ship was too near, as if the distance between it and the Gateway had somehow diminished when no one was looking.

And yet the test circuits on the detector showed no malfunction, no error. All he could do would be to make a report to the maintenance section when he got back.

He was about to move on when something caught his attention.

A sound? Out here? He strained to listen.

Master? Orders, master?

The Doctor's mobile computer was chugging towards him across the void. 'Orders, master?' it repeated.

Lane looked around, as if there was a slim possibility that K-9 might be talking to somebody else. 'What do you want?' he said.

'Efficiency rating five hundred per cent and rising,' K-9 said happily. 'Batten down the hatches and serve every robot an extra tot of oil. Who left the spanner in the lightsail rigger's sump?'

'You've got the wrong man,' Lane said, and he tried to back away.

K-9 rolled after him. 'Please check indicators on all seals before blowing airlocks.'

'Get lost.'

'Hold the aerosol upright. Not for use in vacuum or non-gravity situations.'

'Don't follow me.'

'Orders, master.'

'That was an order.'

'Doctor's orders. An apple a day keeps blob fungus away.'

'Stop following me.'

But as Lane did his best to ignore the distraction

and plot his way back to the privateer, K-9 wouldn't stop following him. And he wouldn't shut up, either.

The Deep Freeze, the crew called it, although the temperature was only a few degrees lower than the rest of the ship. The slaves lay crammed together in ranks on three-tier shelving, arranged alternately head to foot. Each was linked to a cluster of tubes which supplied breathing mixture, intravenous food and the system-depressants that kept their bodies inert. The tubes were linked to main umbilicals that drooped between retaining rings on the uppermost tier.

The shelving lined both sides of the narrow hold, deep into the ship. There was a walkway down the middle, a raised grille that was lit from underneath. It threw a pattern of shadow-squares that made Sagan look almost demonic as he said, 'Want to pick one you like?'

Dulles started to inspect each of the slaves in turn, assuming that Sagan meant it. Each one was tightly chained, a chill fog of condensation drifting around each body. Dulles swallowed nervously.

'Over here,' Sagan said. He was on the other side of the hold, looking at the plastic card from the slot identifying the slave in that position. 'Name's Laszlo, for what it's worth. Let's see if we can get him woken up without wasting him.'

Dulles went back to get the wheeled transport

wagon to carry the slave away, and Sagan began disconnecting the feed tubes.

This is a waste of time, he thought. *I've never seen an onboard revival yet that wasn't fatal.*

Romana was thinking about Gallifrey, and this angered her.

Gallifrey was the home planet of the Time Lords, the home of Romana and once – although she sometimes found it difficult to believe – the home of the Doctor himself. That belief wasn't easy because the Doctor seemed to be the very soul of nonconformity, while the Time Lords as a race were ... well, very worthy, but dull.

The reason for her anger? Gallifrey kept pushing its way back into her thoughts, claiming her attention while she tried to concentrate on the problem of the void. No matter what deductive method she tried to apply to her problem, everything failed for lack of information and then Gallifrey, the world that she'd been hoping never to see again, would rise in her thoughts, unbidden.

Her time with the Doctor had been an eventful apprenticeship in real-universe living, but now – thanks to a summons from their home planet – it was coming to an end. They'd been on their way back when they'd unwittingly crossed into E-Space, and most of their efforts since that time had been directed to getting out.

Well, they were out. But in a reality that was neither one place nor the other.

Zero coordinates. A place of no space, of no time, a pocket of being that ought to exist only as a theory, a numerical tool, a mathematical convenience . . .

'Hello,' Adric said. 'Get yourself lost?'

She spun round in surprise and choked back the urge to squeak with delight. By some fluke, her wandering must have brought her back to—

Romana frowned. 'Where's the TARDIS?' she said.

Adric was standing a few feet away. He flipped his token casually, caught it, flipped it again. 'There's no such thing as where in the void,' he said, 'that's what the Doctor was explaining. You create the place by being there.'

'You mean you left the TARDIS after I gave you specific instructions to stay?'

'I thought you'd be pleased I found you.'

'Found me? Now you've succeeded in losing two of us.'

'*I'm* not lost,' Adric said patiently.

'So how do you propose we get back?'

'Same way I got here.' Flip. 'Let the coin decide.'

Gold on white, it sparkled hypnotically as it spun. Adric picked it out of the air. 'It works, Romana, really. Just like the Doctor said it would.'

'You shouldn't always take the Doctor too seriously. Sometimes he argues for the sake of it.'

'It doesn't matter. I checked out the probabilities and got sixty per cent accuracy. Expand the sample enough, and you can cancel that out.'

'And you believe that works?' Romana said.

'It led me to you, didn't it?' Adric said.

He flipped the coin twice. The first toss to determine an axis of movement, the second to choose a direction. Satisfied, he faced left and started to move off. In a while she'd see him go through the same process again, repeating the sequence as he narrowed in on his imagined target.

'But you came this way,' Romana said, pointing, but even as she raised her hand she realised that she wasn't sure. Spin round a couple of times in the void, and your sense of direction could go completely.

'It doesn't matter,' Adric said.

Despite of her lack of faith in the method, Romana followed.

Back in the banqueting hall, the first event to catch everybody's attention since the Doctor's questioning of the Gundan was the arrival of Pieman Joe from the privateer. He brought the crew's lunch.

He staggered down the steps from the entrance tunnel. As well as carrying a mass detector he was laden with a large box that had a hinged lid and a handle. He was ready to drop in his tracks. He headed towards the banqueting table and yelled, 'Lunch!' so everyone would hear.

He lifted the box with a final effort, and slammed it onto the table. The impact raised a cloud of dust and he tottered back, coughing.

The crew appeared as if by magic. The first one to the box opened the lid and they all gathered round, clucking and cooing: *lunch, great, what have we got, it's about time, I'm just ready . . .*

Rorvik was glancing around as he stepped in amongst them. The Doctor hadn't appeared yet, and Rorvik wanted to be sure that he didn't hear what was about to be said. Bad strategy.

'Right, lads.' Rorvik kept his voice low. 'Since the Doctor isn't here yet, I just want to grab this opportunity of us being all here together to say something. Now, you all know about the problem we've had with the warp motors, and why we're trapped here in the . . .'

It had slowly dawned on Rorvik that nobody was paying him any attention at all. He couldn't compete with the lunchbox. He walked round the table, shouldered in between two crewmen, and slammed the lid. The general appreciative muttering became a little chorus of disappointment. He held down the lid and glared around. 'I'm only going to say this once.'

Somebody muttered, 'Good', and Rorvik shot him a withering glance before continuing.

'We've got no warp motors and no navigator. In practical terms, it means we stay here for ever. That's unless we can fix one and replace the other.'

Nestor said, 'How do you replace the warp motor?' and Rorvik looked heavenward in a plea for patience.

'We replace Biroc. We revive as many of the Tharil slaves as we have to until we get one that survives the procedure. As for the warp motors, that's where the Doctor comes in.'

Jos said, 'Will he be so keen when he finds out we're a slave ship?'

'Or,' Nestor added, 'that the motors got damaged in a blast from an Antonine scout?'

Rorvik thought about pointing out that the Doctor's background might not even have given him knowledge of the anti-slavery alliance, but he simply said, 'If he's got an ounce of scruple, of course he won't be keen. That's why we'll force him to help us. Any questions?'

Clearly there was only one question in everybody's mind, but no one would come out and say it. Rorvik glared around; they were all staring longingly at the lunch box. He took his hands away, and the chatter resumed.

WARP SYSTEMS POWERED DOWN

OVERLOAD SYSTEMS POWERED DOWN

LIFE-SUPPORT HOLDING AT PLANETFALL LEVELS

REC ROOM COFFEE DISPENSER NOW INOPERABLE

ELECTRICAL SYSTEMS FAILURES IN REC ROOM

UNDERFLOOR CABLING

WARNING: NO NEW INFORMATION ON PRESENT
LOCATION COORDINATES SEE 01/00/2222 FOR SYSTEMS
CHECK

WARNING: POSSIBLE UNDETECTED FAULT IN
EXTERIOR SENSORY APPARATUS
AM I IN NEED OF A SERVICE, OR IS THIS SHIP
GETTING SMALLER?

Adric's idea had been to head back to the TARDIS, but somehow the privateer had got in the way. He knew nothing of the warning that the ship's inboard computer was showing to the crew, and which the crew were ignoring, nor of the readings from Lane's mass detector showing the distance between the privateer and the Gateway to be contracting.

All he knew was that he and Romana were standing under the privateer's jutting fin, and it seemed to make a mighty mess of his theory.

Something else had made a mighty mess of the privateer.

The damaged section was a little way along from the engine shells. The edges had been pushed into the hole, and the surrounding metal was blackened and soot-streaked.

'The Doctor didn't mention this,' Adric said.

Romana nodded. There was no obvious access to the ship anywhere near. If the Doctor had been brought in on the other side, there was no way that he could have seen the damage.

Romana said, 'Perhaps they didn't say anything about it,' but the idea made her uneasy. It was obvious evidence of a missile hit. 'Somebody was chasing them,' she said. 'I wonder why?'

Adric had already pocketed his token and was at the rent in the hull. The lower edge was a good step up, just reachable. 'Let's find out,' he said, and he'd pulled himself inside before Romana could argue.

She followed, instead.

It was comparatively dark inside, and it took her eyes a moment to adjust. She paused on the threshold of the tear, and the first feature that she saw clearly in the gloom was Adric's hand, stretched out to help her up.

'I can manage, thank you,' she said coldly, and climbed up beside him.

They were in a sealed area between the inner and outer skins of the privateer. There wasn't much room to move around. About fifteen feet above them there was a catwalk, reached by a sloping maze of equipment, wiring, piping, and conduit. There were short cat-ladders for extra assistance. Lighting was intermittent, provided by flashing lights within the equipment banks; there was also a more uneven sparking that indicated a serious fault.

Adric was already halfway up the first cat-ladder.

'Looks like serious damage, doesn't it?' he said. 'Any idea what we're looking at?'

'These are warp motor control circuits, basic Minados design. Any Time Lord could tell you that.'

The Minados design was one of the commonest available, either in original or pirated form, and the Minados sales force was the most efficient in anyone's history. As soon as their prototype motor was completed, they built it into a market research survey ship and sent it to jump out to the galactic fringe and back again. The ship aged a few months, the galaxy a few hundred years; the robot probes then surveyed the number of Minados warps in use and, where possible, identified the users. The information was coded into a tachyon beam and fired at a plotted point in space; as the tachyons could only exist at super-lightspeeds, the message effectively travelled back in time. It was picked up by the Minados people less than a year after the probe's launch. Knowing their customers before the customers knew it themselves allowed the manufacturers to avoid overproduction and wasteful sales campaigning.

Piracy of the design was less of a problem than it might have been. Minados set up its own piracy operations and stole its own design – much neater, and it kept everyone happy.

As Romana had said, any Time Lord would be familiar with the story.

'So does that mean you're a Time Lord, too?' Adric asked her.

Romana said carefully, 'By training, perhaps. By temperament, no.'

Adric reached the catwalk and swung round to sit on it and look down. 'But I heard the Doctor say that you'd be going back to Gallifrey.'

'That is the idea.' Romana came up beside him and dusted off her hands.

Adric was getting the message; drop the subject. He looked around. 'Why do you think they were being chased?'

'I don't know.'

Adric scrambled to his feet and moved off down the catwalk. It ended at a service airlock to the main hull of the privateer. On the metal bulkhead next to the door was a simple touch-panel and sensor arrangement, to monitor air pressures and deadlock the doors against the ship being inadvertently opened to vacuum.

He glanced back. Romana wasn't watching. He touched the panel. Obviously the deadlocks were disengaged. The door slid open immediately.

From within the privateer, muted by the obstruction of the further airlock door, there came a drawn-out howl of agony.

Romana looked up at the sound, but already it was

being shut off; Adric was in the airlock and the door on her side was closing. She ran down the catwalk and hit the touch-panel, but there was a delay as the lock went through its cycle; the other door had to close before this one would re-open.

She came out into a darkened room, low-ceilinged and an irregular shape. There were storage boxes stacked around, and an elongated grid of light was thrown across them from a grille in one bulkhead wall. The howling was louder and more distressing here, perhaps as near as the next room.

Adric was pushing one of the boxes across to the grille so that he could stand on it and look through.

The situation didn't allow for a reprimand – at least, not yet. Romana crossed the storeroom and climbed up beside him.

They were looking down into another, slightly bigger chamber. It was as if they were in the uppermost gallery of an anatomy class.

Several boxes had been pushed together, and on this makeshift table lay a Tharil. *Is it Biroc?* Romana wondered, but no. This alien was taller, slightly thinner. Patches of his fur had been ripped away, and electrodes had been attached. There were also drip-tubes strapped to his arm in such a way that he couldn't shake them off. Two crewmen stood, one either side. As Romana and Adric watched, the Tharil suddenly came bolt upright, straining against the cables and straps. There were curls of smoke from where electrodes touched bare skin.

The two crewmen gripped a shoulder each and wrestled the Tharil down. They were careful not to come into contact with any of the cables.

The howling continued, and the Tharil started to convulse.

As he shook, his outline started to shimmer. One of the crewmen, the com-point headset of a communications clerk hanging from his belt, started to curse.

'Forget it,' he said. 'We've lost this one.'

The sounds of agony were now no more than a strangled gurgle. The Tharil lay still as the other crewman shut down the power, and soon the noise stopped altogether.

The communications clerk, sleeves rolled up, was wiping his hands on a towel. He was also shaking his head at his failure.

The other crewman was bringing an empty trolley. 'Why does it hurt them so much?'

'Because they're Tharils.' The communications clerk's voice carried clearly up to the grille. 'They're not like you and me – we've got a fixed existence in space and time, they haven't. It's like they never quite made it into another world. Try to tie them down, and it's agony.'

'Like the way Biroc used to howl when we chained him.'

The clerk threw the towel down. 'Don't waste your sympathy,' he said, 'they're only slaves. Come on, we'll try another.'

They pushed the trolley through the sliding doors and out into the corridor. Romana could hear Adric climbing down off the box beside her and moving away to look through some of the adjoining storerooms, but she stayed to watch the Tharil.

It was pointless; the Tharil obviously wasn't capable of anything more. His temporal instability increased and waned but didn't show any signs of becoming steady. She was about to turn and follow Adric when a hand like a vice clamped onto her wrist.

'I don't know where you came from,' Packard said, 'but give me three guesses.'

Packard didn't know who the young woman was, but she had to be from the Doctor's craft. The damage report on the warp control circuits would have to wait – here was more of a prize, and perhaps the leverage they would need to secure the Doctor's complete cooperation. If there had been any doubt that the Doctor might be of use to them, that doubt was now gone; if he'd concealed the fact that he wasn't alone, then he was probably concealing more.

He pulled the woman down from the box. She started to step towards him, to get her balance, and he immediately knew that she'd be no easy captive; she was lining up a combat move, and he couldn't afford to let her.

The only way out would be to use his strength to keep her off-balance, keep her moving so she couldn't use his own weight and power against him. He pulled her towards the main corridor, so she either had to stagger after or fall.

Packard dragged his new prisoner out into the upper storeroom access corridor and down the ironwork steps to the main level, round a corner and past two doors to stop at a third: Sagan's recovery room. The mounting number of dead Tharils would be company for her, and a clear sign that it made good sense to be obedient.

As soon as she was inside and the door had closed, he coded it to lock.

Alone in the corridor, he took a breath. He didn't get enough exercise, and when he got it he didn't much like it. He looked up to see Lane coming from the direction of the bridge.

'I just got back,' Lane said. 'Someone said you were looking for me.'

'You were supposed to help Sagan but forget it.' The scan-surveys of the Doctor's craft were no longer important, the anomalies of no consequence. 'See to this, instead,' he said, and held out the clipboard that he'd been carrying under his arm.

'What is it?'

'Damage checklist for the warp motor. Let me know when it's finished.'

Having offloaded the job, Packard walked off briskly, other things on his mind.

Lane looked at the clipboard and moved off in the direction of the warp access hatch, not quite so eager.

It was obvious to Rorvik that nothing was going to be accomplished at the gateway until the lunchbreak was over. He could threaten and he could coerce, but the cooperation he'd get would be resentful and only half-attentive.

The crew had dusted off one end of the banqueting table and set out their meal, as civilised as anyone could wish considering the circumstances. Rorvik watched, incredulous.

'Finished?' he said at last with suppressed anger.

The crewmen nodded and smiled appreciatively. If there was irony there, they were insensitive to it. A couple of them were wiping their lips with napkins. Another burped.

'Then,' Rorvik said, 'would you mind getting off your backsides and finding the Doctor for me?'

'We know he's around here, somewhere,' Nestor said.

'Around here somewhere isn't good enough! I want an armed guard and I want him marched back to the ship!'

The crewmen shrugged and carried on getting themselves ready without any particular haste; dusting off crumbs, unholstering their sidearms, checking the charges that they carried. One man blew his nose.

Rorvik watched for a few seconds. Then he unholstered his own sidearm.

He aimed at the centre of the lunchtime debris on the table.

There was a crack, and a bright flash of light that illuminated the entire banqueting hall for perhaps half a second; napkins, bones and crumpled drinks cans jumped high into the air and came clattering down.

They all stared at Rorvik, open-mouthed.

(If they'd glanced up to the minstrel's gallery, they'd have seen the Doctor, candelabrum in hand, making a quiet assessment of the scene that he'd just witnessed. But they didn't. Nor did they see him nod sagely to himself, set the candelabrum down at the top of the gallery stairs, and back off into the labyrinth of upper corridors.)

'Move!' their captain roared. 'Bring them in!'

Rorvik watched his men scatter, brandishing his gun and playing the pirate chieftain. Then he hesitated; he did a quick mental calculation and looked around.

There was a crash from the minstrels' gallery as someone fell over something. Rorvik was momentarily distracted, but he only glanced up as he strode to the far end of the table. He lifted the linen cloth, old and frail and brittle. He looked underneath.

Nestor was hiding there, fingers in his ears; after a moment, he realised that he was being observed.

'Any sign of him down there?' asked Rorvik.

Nestor grinned, nervously and somewhat sheepishly.

Adric had been coming back from another unlit part of the storeroom complex when he'd seen Packard with Romana and stepped back into the shadows. Neither had been aware of him as they passed. Adric's first idea had been to follow Romana and to set her loose at the first opportunity,, but with the need to stay out of sight he soon lost the trail. He tried to backtrack but must have taken another wrong turn. It was then that he heard voices coming his way, and saw shadows thrown on the far wall at an intersection.

He backed into cover, and cautiously peeked round the corner.

There were two of them, both about the same size, both noticeably older than any of the other crew, and they both wore similar pull-on knitted caps. Between them they were pulling a black plastic garbage bag.

'So I cleaned it off,' one of them was saying.

'Did you?'

'Cleaned it off and replaced that little collar around the end, and it was as good as anything. Still got it.'

'And they'd thrown it away, just like that?'

'Just like that.'

'They don't know the value of anything.'

They were getting close enough for Adric to be able to read the nametags on their coveralls. One was called Aldo, the other Waldo. Adric was starting to think that maybe they wouldn't turn out to be much of a threat when another crewman appeared around the corner. He was carrying a clipboard, his name tag read Lane, and he didn't look so harmless.

'Sagan's looking for you,' Aldo said as Lane came level.

Lane was more interested in the listing on the clip-board. 'I know,' he said.

'He's waking up slaves,' Waldo added.

Lane said, 'I know.'

Another howling was starting up; this one was close, somewhere in the corridors.

'Killing 'em off, more like,' Aldo said.

Lane said, 'Yes, I know.' He was past them now, and not really listening; Waldo peered after him, and decided to see how much he could get away with.

'You've got a pointed 'ead.'

'Yes,' Lane said absently, 'I know.'

Aldo and Waldo shared a secret giggle behind Lane's back; this turned into what looked to be near panic as Lane stopped in his tracks. Adric felt a sudden stab of fear, supposing he'd been discovered; but that wasn't the case, not yet, at least. Lane was walking back towards the two crewmen, who were now busying themselves tipping the contents of the garbage bag into a slide-back waste point in the corridor wall.

'Something puzzles me,' Lane said.

'Oh, yes?' Aldo said with exaggerated innocence. Or perhaps it was Waldo – at a distance it was difficult to tell.

'Yes.' He indicated the waste point. 'Where does all this stuff go?'

Waldo started to recite. 'Every shift we do the bridge and the communal areas. Every second shift we do the bunkrooms and the kitchens. Every third shift the engine rooms and the corridor waste points, and once a tour we give every bin a spray of disinfectant.'

'Yes,' Lane said, 'but where does it all go?'

'Go?' echoed Waldo.

'Where does what go?' added Aldo.

Lane indicated the rubbish again. 'It can't just build up for ever.'

Aldo glanced at Waldo, and then winked at Lane. 'Trade secret,' he said.

They were already moving off, dragging the near-empty bag and muttering to each other. At the intersection, the muttering turned again to cackling laughter. Lane watched them go; then he shook his head, as if to clear it.

Time to back off, Adric thought, and he turned to move away.

The corridor he'd ducked into was about fifteen feet long, with a dead end.

At the end was a door. Making no sound, Adric padded to it and touched the slide control on the wall alongside. Nothing happened; it required a number code to key it open. He desperately tried a couple of three-figure combinations, but he knew that it was hopeless; he'd no chance of hitting the right pattern in the few seconds it would take for Lane to appear around the corner.

No chance? No chance at all?

He took the token from his pocket.

The howling stopped around the same time that Lane was stopping to bang one of the corridor light fittings with the edge of the clipboard. Some of the bulbs were blown completely, but in many cases it was simply a bad connection and a little jarring would bring the lights on again. But not this time.

Sagan and Dulles came round the corner. Dulles was pushing the slave trolley and contributing most of the effort while Sagan was making a show of pulling it. There was a form on the trolley, fully covered by a loose tarpaulin. The tarpaulin wasn't very clean.

Lane said, 'How's it going?'

'Badly,' Sagan said wearily. 'Where were you when I needed you?'

'Running errands for Packard. What's the problem?'

'You can't revive a Tharil without a decently equipped revival room, that's the problem. Look at this.' He drew back the tarpaulin. There was a Tharil underneath, its outline shimmering spasmodically. 'Unstable. Useless. A fortune in any currency you care to name, no navigators like them in the known universe. This is the second we've wasted – three, if you count Biroc. Are you here to help me now?'

Lane shook his head. 'Dealing with this,' he said, and held up the clipboard.

Sagan dropped the tarpaulin back over the wasted Tharil, looked at Dulles and sighed heavily. Then he thought of something else.

'I just talked to the bridge,' he said. 'You know Packard found a woman?'

'Lucky Packard.'

'On the ship, I mean. Reckons she's with the Doctor. So that's his cooperation guaranteed, now!'

'Sure,' Lane said as they wheeled the trolley past him, although he really wasn't certain he understood at all. But he was just a humble artisan, as Rorvik was always fond of telling him, and shouldn't be expected to understand matters of such depth and complexity.

Romana heard the locking mechanism disengage before the door opened, so she was already looking up when Sagan and the trolley with the second Tharil came in.

She was sitting on an upturned box. She was a little less tense now she knew that the prostrate alien on the makeshift table was no threat. The Tharil's name was – or had been – Laszlo. She learned as much from a small plastic card that had dropped to the floor from the bench. He still shimmered, and didn't move.

Romana stood up and backed off as the trolley approached; Sagan grinned, and looked her over. 'Brought you another friend,' he said. 'But don't expect much in the way of conversation.'

Dulles pushed together a few more boxes, and the two of them transferred the new Tharil across. Then they wheeled the trolley out, and Sagan paused to re-secure the door. The last Romana saw of him was his grin, as he leaned with the sliding edge to keep it in view as long as possible.

A man convinced of his own charm, she thought, briefly entertaining the idea of making an effort to win him over. But that was for wet heroines in improbable stories, the kind she'd never been able to take seriously. She turned her back on Laszlo and moved across to the new Tharil. This one hadn't even made it far enough to be tortured. Perhaps he was lucky.

(She was so absorbed that she didn't hear the gentle slither of fur across metal behind her.)

Romana turned his plastic ID card over in her

hands. There was other information, but not in any form that she could understand. The new time-sensitive was named Geis. He wasn't dead but didn't look as if he'd last much longer. He was shorter and slightly heavier than either Biroc or Laszlo, and his aura was starting to break up.

Suddenly the Tharil's outline heaved, and his body stiffened. The glow that surrounded him pulsed once, impossibly bright, and then faded completely.

A time sensitive. Was this how it ended for them? With no future options open, no choice of timelines to pull at his material body, this Tharil had simply ... ceased to be?

Romana turned away, and found herself looking up into Laszlo's brutally scarred face.

Over at the Gateway, Nestor stayed with Jos in the search for the Doctor. This was in the hope that, should there be any shooting or hard talking to be done, Jos would handle the worst of it. Jos stayed with Nestor for most of the same reasons.

Both were encouraged by the fact that they were armed and the Doctor wasn't. They were even more encouraged by the fact the Rorvik was behind them, in spirit if not in immediate physical presence, and fear of his annoyance made most risks seem preferable.

So, when they saw the Doctor at the far end of a passageway, they didn't hesitate too long in their surprise.

Only long enough for him to dodge sideways through an arch, and then they were following.

They crammed into the doorway at the same time; it wasn't quite wide enough and they stuck there, struggling shoulder to shoulder. After a couple of seconds they popped through like champagne corks.

They'd been led into a darkened chamber where the only illumination was the shaft of light from the passageway behind them. The Doctor was framed squarely in the beam, looking frantically around with nowhere to run; he was almost making it easy for them. They piled forward to grab him . . .

. . . and bounced off the mirrored force field in which they'd seen him reflected.

As they tumbled in a disorganised heap, the Doctor stepped over and past them to get back to the corridor.

But there Rorvik was waiting, gun held high.

'Now, Doctor,' Rorvik said, and let rip a couple of shots into the ceiling; the noise thundered through the passageways, and dust and plaster showered down.

It wasn't subtle, but it was effective. The Doctor skidded to a stop. Rorvik, his point made, now levelled the gun.

'Steady on, old chap,' the Doctor said, 'those things can be dangerous.'

'Too right they can, Doctor. So, let's see a little cooperation.'

The Doctor started backing off into the side-chamber. The two crewmen who'd followed him were on their feet, looking embarrassed.

The Doctor said to Rorvik, 'What kind of cooperation did you have in mind?'

'A little sympathy and understanding for a bunch of helpless travellers in distress.' Rorvik was following, keeping the Doctor well within range. 'And some straight answers. What do you know about those mirrors?'

'Oh,' said the Doctor, almost backed up to the mirror, 'not a lot . . .'

Rorvik cut across the diffident denial with another blast into the ceiling, another snowfall of plaster.

'This could be a listed building for all you know,' the Doctor protested, but Rorvik let off another blast, and this one was close; so close that the Doctor had to crouch back and cover his head with his good hand.

He tried to tell Rorvik that threats and damage weren't going to get him anywhere, but had to duck from another blast that was even closer – how many charges could these pistols hold? Flying stone chips picked at his skin, and he stumbled; he had to put out his damaged hand to steady himself against the mirror.

It all happened in an instant.

The Doctor pitched backward, into his own reflection and through.

Rorvik started to reach out, but it was too late. The

Doctor's scarf dropped to the floor, but no Doctor fell with it.

Rorvik touched the mirror. It was solid, impassable. He was momentarily numb with amazement, too taken aback at the stupendous mess he'd made of the operation to show any anger. He crouched down and picked up the scarf; weighing it in his hand, he again looked into the mirror.

Only his reflection looked back.

Romana took a step back, and tried to get out of the Tharil's reach; but she came up against the bench where Geis had expired, and could retreat no further. Laszlo quickly raised a reassuring hand. His aura flickered and then died; it was obviously an effort for him. He said, 'You are no slaver. Laszlo will not harm you.'

'I . . . I thought you were dying,' Romana said.

The Tharil certainly seemed to be in a bad way; the fur on one side of his face had been scorched and blackened, and an eye was nearly closed by the bruised tissue around it.

He said, 'Laszlo thought so, too. But Laszlo survives.' And he stepped back, so that Romana might no longer feel threatened.

So, he didn't consider her to be a slaver; that, at least, explained the true nature of the privateer and its crew, and perhaps the missile damage in the hull if they'd tried to run some blockade.

She said, 'I'm Romana.'

'Slave?' said Laszlo, who had obviously never heard of the slavers trading in their own kind.

'More of a hostage. These people are in a bad situation. Their warp motors are damaged, and they're ... *we* are trapped in the void outside space and time.'

'But why should they wake Laszlo?'

'Because Biroc escaped ...'

Laszlo's reaction to the name was swift. '*Biroc?* Biroc lives?' And for a moment he lost the effort of control, and began to shimmer; seen so close, the nature of the aura was apparent – it was as if several different forms of the creature were co-existing within the same shell, and each was straining to break out and follow a separate destiny.

Romana said, 'You're time sensitives, yes? That's the only explanation for what I've seen.'

'We are Tharils. We ride the time waves, we sense the winds of change. Because of this, we are hunted and sold to be chained. But if Biroc runs free ...'

'Nobody knows where he went.'

'Laszlo will find. Laszlo will follow.'

'Laszlo hasn't got a hope. Look around, we're still prisoners.'

The Tharil drew himself up, and for a moment the bearing of the slave had the arrogance of a king. He held out his hand; it was like a lion's paw, the claws slightly extended.

Romana eyed it nervously, but it was palm-up, non-threatening.

'Give Laszlo your hand,' he said.

Romana, fascinated by the outstretched paw, didn't understand at first. Laszlo made a slight beckoning motion; and then she raised her hand uncertainly and placed it in the Tharil's palm.

Laszlo's outline remained crisp and clear, but the room around them began to shimmer as the Tharil had done; it took her a moment to realise why.

Laszlo was pulling her out of phase.

Back in the small chamber above the banqueting hall, Rorvik was dealing with his annoyance the best way he knew how. He was taking it out on those around him, starting with Nestor, who had the misfortune of being nearest.

'Do you know what you've done?' he roared. 'He wasn't supposed to get past you, and you let him!' Rorvik turned to Jos. 'Are you happy? Are you satisfied now – now that we've lost our only chance of getting the warp motors fixed? Do you really feel that your life's been a success?'

A couple of the other crewmen had arrived by now, attracted by the noise. They watched uncomfortably from the open doorway.

Finding Nestor and Jos unsatisfactory targets, Rorvik turned to the mirrored arch and raised his voice.

'Can you hear me, Doctor? I've got a message for you: I hate you. Did you get that? Of everybody I've ever met, you're my least favourite!'

And he hammered his fists on the mirror's surface in frustration.

The Doctor was not, in fact, hearing Rorvik, although he could see the slaver captain perfectly well. No sound passed through the mirror, and from this side it wasn't a mirror at all; it was clear air, and Rorvik appeared to be drumming his fists on nothing.

The floor looked like stone, but it was warm and not too rough. The Doctor pushed himself up to sit with his back against the wall; he'd landed heavily, not knowing what was ahead, and he'd bruised his hand although it didn't feel as if anything was broken. He'd been rubbing it for a few seconds before he realised that anything was wrong.

Or rather, it wasn't. The hand that had been blasted and aged by the time winds was now whole. He turned it round but there was no sign of temporal scarring, and when he pulled back his sleeve and rolled back the cuff of his shirt there was no spread of damage.

He'd touched the mirror before but never with this hand, the hand that had passed through the time winds. The touch of this hand had been the key; once through, it was restored.

The Doctor hurriedly dug in his pocket, looking

around as he did so. This part of the Gateway was hardly different to the other areas that he'd seen, except that it was cleaner, somehow brighter, and when he looked down the passage he saw another difference; its end couldn't be seen, lost in the void fog.

He brought out the memory wafers that he'd taken from K-9. He'd so far been unable to find anything that could match them, although to see the wafers now it was difficult to see why it had been necessary; he rubbed them, flexed them, tapped them together, and they didn't crumble.

Passage through the mirror had restored them, as it had restored him.

Now, if K-9 could somehow be brought across . . .

The Doctor glanced at Rorvik. The captain's temper hadn't improved, but he'd stopped taking it out on the mirror. Now he was giving instructions to his men, but his back was turned so that there was no point even trying to lip-read. Whatever he was saying, the Doctor could infer the obvious message; forget any immediate attempt to pass back through the mirror.

There was a distant whine, the clicking of servo motors. He looked around.

From the void mists of the corridor, the Gundan emerged. Instead of the dusty and aged relic that the Doctor had last seen, the war machine was now slick and gleaming. It still carried the axe and moved with a smooth assurance that was somehow more than mechanical.

It stopped.

After a few moments, the Doctor felt his apprehension subside; the Gundan was no longer mindlessly attacking but seemed to be looking for something. It turned its head slightly, as if it could hear.

'Gundan!' the Doctor called. 'Are you hearing me?'

No response. The Doctor held up the restored memory wafer in his made-over hand. 'The time winds get you through the mirrors, and the Gateway heals the damage. Am I right?'

Ignoring the Doctor's words, the Gundan seemed satisfied enough to dismiss him. It turned and stepped forward into the corridor wall; instead of crashing into the stonework it melted through like a ghost.

Again, the Doctor was alone.

'At least tell me how I get back!' he called after, but there was nothing to give him a reply.

Lane was carrying out the order, given to him by Packard, to assess the damage in the warp motor control circuits using the troubleshooting list in the ship's manual.

It wasn't easy; the privateer had seen long service and its maintenance history was, at best, erratic. He started going wrong on item three, when a cable that was supposedly an essential part of an overload-absorption circuit was traced through to end in a neatly tied knot that connected to nothing at all. After that it got worse; the Minados colour codes had been ignored when new material had been installed, and some repairs were obviously in-flight jerry rigs that had been left to work on the principle of That Which Ain't Broke Need Nary Be Fixed.

He got to item nine, with only three ticks against the list. It had degenerated into no more than a formality, of no practical use at all; what the bridge really needed to know could be told at a glance.

He wedged the clipboard and checklist in between two thick ropes of cable for some other poor sucker to follow through and climbed the cat-ladders to the intercom point on the upper gangway.

Adric felt a knot of fear loosen as he crouched under the gangway, watching the crewman through the mesh grille of the flooring overhead. The man suspected nothing.

'Packard? It's Lane,' the man was telling the bridge. 'Down in the warp control section. It could be worse than we thought.'

'What do you mean?' came Packard's reply, made tinny by the cheap wall speaker.

'The missile hit, it didn't only break the skin and jinx the warp controls. Some of the main power routings are uncovered.'

'Is that serious?'

'Could be, if you believe the handbook. A few more inches, and we'd lose all our drive power.'

110

'Well, as long as we didn't—'

Adric saw the man jump as the exchange was cut short by the sudden and strident blare of an electronic alarm as the overhead lights plunged to a deep red. The noise from the speaker could only be heard as a distorted babble, impossible to make out. But Lane would know well enough what such an alarm meant: condition red, major alert, and if he didn't get back inside fast the ship would be sealed and he'd be stranded on the wrong side of the door. He stepped in quickly, operated the control, and was gone.

Sagan had triggered the red alert – Laszlo and the woman were on their way out with nobody to stop them, and both were out of phase.

He'd been flung against the wall, and Dulles hurled halfway down the corridor. After he'd reached the alarm handle in its wall recess and ensured that everybody else's day got ruined, too, Sagan fumbled out his pistol.

Unfortunately (for him) he was a terrible shot. Of the three charges that he put after Laszlo and Romana, two of them put out lights, and the third blew open a waste pipe from the rec room corridor above and brought down a shower of stale coffee.

Lane saw them next, stopped in his tracks as he rounded a corner in the below-decks complex by the sight of the linked pair bearing down on him, slowed and shimmering like a desert mirage.

Before he could overcome his surprise, they were upon him, sweeping past as Lane bounced from the corridor wall as if it was sprung, propelled by a straight-armed blow from Laszlo. That's how Lane remembered it, more or less, when he could sit upright and think straight again.

On the bridge, Packard was shouting to be heard over the alarms. A fine situation, he was thinking, when a danger signal attracted more attention to itself than it did to the danger.

'Will somebody tell me who's ringing the bells,' he bellowed, 'and why?'

He looked around him helplessly; the crew had been galvanised into a purposeless panic, but there was one crewman at Sagan's communications desk who seemed to be signalling to him. Packard moved over, and the crewman held out the spare comms headset.

Through the earpiece, without knowing whether or not anyone could hear him, Sagan was pouring out a stream of babble.

'*The Tharil*,' Packard heard. '*He was faking! He's out and running, and the woman's with him!*'

Packard didn't wait for the background information. 'Tharil on the loose!' he bellowed across the bridge. 'Seal the ship!'

Sealing the ship was the job of the helmsman. Nestor was the helmsman, and he was out at the Gateway. The helm stood unattended until an inexperienced recruit named Kliban, realising that nobody else was going to take it on, climbed to the compass platform – an archaic name, since they had nothing that resembled a traditional compass – and dropped into the chair.

The privateer had been designed with mutiny in mind, so that the captain could seal himself into the bridge if necessary and take over the ship's major functions from a single central point. The bank of override switches that faced Kliban was enough to make him regret his decision. He reached out, and tentatively flicked a few of them over.

Adric was on his way down the cat-ladder to the hole in the privateer's side when he heard the emergency bolts slam home in the airlock. The compartment was now cut off from the ship, but fortunately it no longer mattered; he was on the side where he needed to be. He continued his descent.

By this time, Packard had joined Kliban at the helm and was looking over his shoulder.

'Loading bay doors,' he said, and pointed to the appropriate switch. It was the most important single access and exit point, and the one that a Tharil would make for.

The ramp was almost withdrawn as Laszlo and Romana emerged into the loading bay, and the heavy door was starting to roll down.

They made it under, but only just; Laszlo had to stoop, and the closing edge brushed at his mane – but by then they were out and dropping into the void, falling still hand-in-hand to the ground that was no ground.

The lockdown continued but it was too little, too late. Sagan and Lane joined the rest of the crew on the bridge. Dulles had excused himself and woven off towards the sick bay, where an automated Desk Doctor would listen to his problems and print out the appropriate messages of sympathy.

External cameras showed a successful escape.

Packard said, 'Get a warning out to Rorvik. Tell him they're on their way.'

'Who was the woman?' Lane said.

'That,' Packard said with quiet bitterness, 'was our hostage.'

With the alarms sounding and the bay door sealed, Adric had begun to make his way to the outside. His sense of urgency increased when something started to erupt and spark deep in the warp control mechanism but then, as he squeezed by the strontium dampers, the sparks stopped flying and the alarms died. He'd reached the damaged outer skin of the engine chamber. He assumed himself to be alone there, but he wasn't.

'Unit requesting identification,' a familiar voice slurred. He looked down and saw that K-9's head was poking through the tear in the privateer's side. 'K-9,' he said, 'what are you doing here?'

'Obeying instructions.'

'What instructions?'

'Unit was ordered, quote, *Go find a hole and stick your head in it, you dumb heap of tin*, unquote. Analysis indicates that identification of the Doctor was mistaken.'

'Sounds like you were following one of the crew,' Adric said as he climbed out through the rent and over the mobile computer. 'K-9, I need your help.'

'Help?' K-9 queried, slurring again.

'We're on a slave ship.' He took hold of K-9's casing and helped the weakened computer to roll back. 'I don't know what to do.'

K-9 was obviously making an effort, but to little effect. 'It is difficult to keep data in an orderly progression . . . logic fails. There are substantial blanks . . .'

By this time, Adric had seen the trailing charger lead and realised; K-9 was barely ticking over. 'I have to get you back to the TARDIS,' he said.

'I do not believe that I can find the TARDIS. I am too weak to search for its mass.'

'This will get us there,' Adric said, producing the golden token. 'Can you move?'

'I will try.'

Adric composed a question in his mind and flipped the coin; and again. 'Straight out,' he announced. 'Come on.'

K-9 tried to follow as he moved out but could only manage a couple of feet. Adric came back and said, 'It's really bad, isn't it?'

'Yes,' K-9 said simply.

'I'm sorry, K-9.'

'It is unrealistic to feel sorry for a machine. A machine feels no pain. But . . .'

'What?'

There wasn't enough power. K-9's head drooped. Adric started to push him in the direction they needed to go, but there was resistance; they moved, but slowly.

Rorvik's efforts to crack his way through the fabric of the Gateway had so far got him nowhere. Their first attempts attacking the mirror itself had proved both ineffectual and downright dangerous; the charges were simply reflected away to send the watching crewmen running. He'd had Nestor crouch by a mirror arch to pump shots into the stonework at its base. This raised a lot of dust, but when the dust settled there was no damage to speak of. Just some surface pitting of the stone, and some powdering of the mortar in the cracks.

'It isn't working,' Nestor said apologetically. 'We need crowbars, something we can lever the stones out with.'

Rorvik stood looking for a moment, his eyes on the stonework and his thoughts miles away. Then he gave a snarl of disgust and turned to walk back to the gallery and the main hall. As he turned he gave Nestor's head a push; Nestor was still on his haunches, and he over-balanced easily. As Nestor sprawled, two crewmen at the door got out of Rorvik's way.

Jos was listening to the hand radio as Rorvik appeared on the gallery; the signal was bad, and he was holding it to his ear in an effort to make out what Packard was saying.

'Captain Rorvik,' he shouted, 'radio message coming through.'

Rorvik didn't acknowledge. He said, loud enough to reach all of the party and bring them out of their alcoves, 'Holiday's over, move yourselves. I want this dusty hole turned upside down. Anything that'll pass for a lever or a crowbar, anything that will crack open the masonry and get us through this tomb to whatever is on the other side of those doorways.'

By now he'd reached the bottom of the stairs, and the crew were scattering to carry out his order. Except for Jos, who waited apprehensively with the radio as his captain moved towards him.

'If anybody wants to duck out of his responsibility to our little community,' Rorvik went on, 'if anybody wants to go and hide under a table,' (this with a searing glance in Nestor's direction) 'well, fine, let him try it on. But remember this! Anybody I catch not pulling his weight will pay a serious price for it!'

He lowered his voice to speak to Jos. 'Now,' he said, 'what's this message?'

'I don't know,' Jos said with embarrassment. 'You were shouting so much, I couldn't hear it.'

Rorvik closed his eyes for a moment. Then a crewman arrived with the first of the potential crowbar-offerings. It was a long, sinuous statue on a heavy base, metallic-looking and about the size of a walking stick. Without even seeming to pay any attention, Rorvik took the statue and slammed it down hard on the table. It broke cleanly in two. Rorvik tossed the truncated stump back to the crewman, who walked off, the pride of discovery instantly deflated.

Rorvik held out his hand, and Jos gave him the radio. 'Packard?' he said into it. 'Are you hearing me, Packard?'

He listened. There was nothing but static; there might have been words scrambled up in the background, but it was impossible to tell. He tossed the radio back to Jos. Nestor was waiting with another potential crowbar.

'I've got a crew of idiots and a shipload of defective equipment,' Rorvik said. 'That's my reward for being the fairest and most enlightened commander on the spaceways.' He took the new bar – some kind of heavy curtain rail – and slammed the table with it. The bar held – but the arrival of Romana and Laszlo prevented him from making any immediate comment.

The doors at the end of the entrance tunnel burst inwards from the void, and the two figures came pounding down the stone incline and into the main banqueting hall. Rorvik had seen Tharil instability many times before, and he recognised it instantly now. But he'd never been aware that it was communicable by touch; for of the two, one was obviously no time-sensitive, but a humanoid being. And a female humanoid, at that.

They were crossing the hall, unobstructed by anything or anybody. The heavy bar was still in Rorvik's hands. He raised it high and stepped out.

As Rorvik swung the bar down, Laszlo's hand came up to meet it in passing.

The clawed fingers barely seemed to brush the metal, but to Rorvik it felt like he'd slammed down hard on an anvil; his shoulders were jolted and his head rang like the prize bell on a test-your-strength machine.

As he gasped and dropped the bar, they carried on past and into the mirror behind him, dissolving through without a sound.

Massaging his wrist, Rorvik watched the figures go with murder in his eyes. Then, as Nestor ran over to help him up, he looked around at the rest of his crew. They were all standing, uncertainly watching.

Rubbish or not, they were all he had.

Rorvik put a reassuring arm round Nestor's trembling shoulders and forced himself to smile. He only wished that he could feel some little part of the confidence that he was showing.

'We're stable,' Romana said, surprised. It had happened suddenly, as they'd emerged through the mirror.

'This is the Gateway,' Laszlo said. 'Nothing is stable, nothing is unstable.'

'What kind of gateway?'

'An interchange of realities. It belongs to the great days of the Tharils, before the hunting and the enslavement. Days that are no more.'

She looked around: a tidy-looking corridor with its end lost in white mist, and a silent view onto the interior of the banqueting hall. 'Where does all this lead?'

'Anywhere,' Laszlo told her, looking off into the mist. 'Everywhere. If you have the art to use it.'

'And have you?'

'It is lost. Laszlo is like . . . a blind man. In a strange room.'

Something suddenly occurred to Romana, and she looked back through the mirror. When last she'd seen the Doctor, he'd been marching off into the void; there was no sign of where he might be, or of what might have befallen him. She told Laszlo of her worry.

'It is Biroc we must find,' Laszlo insisted. 'Biroc is our leader. Biroc will have a plan for the Tharils.'

He took a few steps towards the mist, and then

turned back to the hesitant Romana. He held out his hand, high and imperious; no longer a slave, he was now in his own country.

'Come,' he said. 'Trust Laszlo.'

Under the circumstances, Romana reflected, she had little choice.

If there was any internal consistency to the layout of the Gateway beyond the mirrors, the Doctor couldn't perceive it. He didn't know how long he'd been wandering and suspected that subjective time was of no real value in this territory anyway. He'd emerged from the interior maze of the castle to find himself in the grounds; long abandoned and overgrown, they'd once been formal gardens but now rotted under a watery-pink sky. The house behind him, once palatial, was now in ruins, and all of the greenery and stonework appeared to have been dusted with a light frost. The mists streamed around and through everything, sometimes making revelations but more often concealing.

Any attempt to get familiar with the gardens seemed inevitably to fail. There were broken-down fountains, resting areas with carved stone benches, groves of statuary; at first it seemed that these were all duplicated several times over, each time remodelled in slightly different form, but closer examination showed him that this was not so. What he saw each time was the same place, the same objects, caught at a different stage of decay. Any effort at making sense of the geographical relationships between these slices of time got him nowhere; he would retrace his steps and find that they led him to some area or some phase of the gardens that he hadn't seen before.

At one time he heard laughter, drifting across to him over untrimmed hedges; he followed the sound hopefully to a flat area like a croquet lawn, except that there were low stone pillars instead of hoops and the grass had given way to moss. Although the laughter and the low murmur of conversation carried on around him, the lawn was deserted. One voice, amused at something, almost became a roar; but it was politely checked in time, and turned into a muffled cough and the click of servos.

The Doctor turned sharply. Servo motors had no place, even in this strange picture.

The Gundan stepped into view from the bushes on the far side. It stopped, and turned square-on. One of the unseen partygoers from long past started to make polite applause, and others followed. The Gundan raised its axe slightly as if to show it and began to march across the lawn towards the Doctor.

This time there was no hesitation, no turning aside. The applause started to echo and become bizarre as the mist swirled across the lawn, and still the Gundan ploughed on. The Doctor knew that he ought at least to back off, if not to run . . . but to where?

The Gundan was already losing substance, dissolving

into the tendrils of mist that curled around its body. With a little less than half the distance to go, it faded out altogether.

The Doctor was left with a single voice, solitary laughter. It was mocking and unpleasant.

Laszlo and Romana, elsewhere and elsewhen in the same strange landscape, were having no better fortune. It was Romana who heard the music playing, and Romana who led the way; Laszlo followed a few paces behind, wary and mistrustful.

They emerged into what looked like a copy of the banqueting hall; except that it really was the banqueting hall, clean and fresh and untouched by time. On the table at its centre there were fresh fruit, meat and tureens of soup so hot that they steamed faintly. There was music from the gallery, and around the table there was chatter and conversation – but apart from Romana and Laszlo, the room was empty of people.

'Nothing,' Romana said. 'Again.'

'He is here somewhere. Laszlo knows it.'

'It's hopeless. Even if we find Biroc, there's nothing he could do.'

'Your kind give in easily to despair,' Laszlo observed, without apparent malice.

Romana's pride was stung. 'I don't give in. I simply can't see the point in wasting time and wandering.'

'Your alternative?'

'First, analyse the problem, decide your objectives. Next, check through your resources. Then look for the pattern that will give you a solution, matching one against the other.'

It was all solid theory; why did it sound so hollow as she said it?

'Technical solutions,' Laszlo said dismissively. 'Easy to predict, easy to forestall.'

'What's your alternative?'

'A trust in intuition.'

Now it was Romana's turn to be lofty. 'Guessing games and blind man's buff.'

But Laszlo turned a hard stare onto her. 'Look around you and see the greatness that once was. Tharil greatness, brought down and ruined by your logical thinkers.'

'Apparently intuition was no defence.'

'The day of the Tharils is come,' Laszlo said, moving towards an exit. 'Matters will be different when it is over. We shall find Biroc.'

Romana looked after him, stumped and frustrated; if he wouldn't stick to logic, she couldn't argue with him.

As she left the hall, the music from the gallery ended. There was the sound of polite applause from the table.

It was the Doctor who found Biroc. As he broke through the tall reeds by an artificial pond he saw the

Tharil on the opposite bank, staring down into the water. The pond was stagnant and putrid, but perhaps Biroc was seeing the clearer waters of another day. He looked up at the sound of the Doctor's approach and seemed, for a moment, to be astonished.

'How did you follow Biroc?' he said.

The Doctor held up his rejuvenated hand and flexed his fingers. 'Good fortune and a brief exposure to the winds of change.'

'Go back. There is nothing for you here.'

'I'd tend to agree. But it's easier said than done.' There was no obvious way of getting across the water. He couldn't see how deep it was and didn't much take to the idea of finding out.

Biroc said, 'The mirrors offer resistance in one direction only.'

'Look,' the Doctor said, 'there's more at stake than just getting everybody back into the lifeboats. When you hijacked the TARDIS, you dropped us in the void with no guidebook.'

'Biroc knows what he is doing.'

'Well, I wish I had his confidence. You're needed . . .'

'By Rorvik? Biroc spits.'

'Use the bargaining power you've got. He does need you.'

'He needs Biroc's kind in chains! That is the only bargain that Rorvik will contemplate. To him we are Tharils, a savage curiosity, beings without feelings or

125

souls, with no redeeming feature other than a price . . . and an occasional usefulness. There will be no bargains with Rorvik.'

'In that case,' the Doctor persisted, 'all he'll have to do will be to chain another slave in your place. You'll lose your one advantage.'

'Rorvik offers nothing.'

'Not even his cargo for his life?'

'Not even that. Biroc will see the Tharils freed, and no deal for Rorvik. Go back. Wait.'

And he turned and walked away from the bank.

The Doctor called after him, 'Go back where?'

Biroc stopped, half-turned, and raised his arm to point. Then he walked on and was swallowed by the overgrowth of a formal maze.

'And wait for what?'

To that, there was no reply.

It wasn't much of a guide, but it would have to do. The Tharil had seemed unworried, the Doctor thought, oddly confident, as if he'd already seen what was set to happen and knew how it would end.

It was a sad kind of courage.

Laszlo brought Romana to a crumbling fountain, overgrown with pale moss. Even though it was broken and dry, there was still the sound of flowing water; the clash of realities was disturbing.

'Forget it, Laszlo,' Romana said to him as he looked

into the fountain's empty bowl. He seemed disappointed, as if he'd expected something more. 'Your Gateway's defunct, and you know it.'

'Do not be misled by details. Details are nothing.'

'We've seen nowhere that hasn't been broken down and deserted. Those who deny reality usually suffer by it in the end. I can see how the Tharils became slaves.'

Laszlo turned suddenly, as if stung. He stared at Romana, and she tried to soften the bitter message a little.

'You trust too much,' she said. 'Now you're relying on Biroc to work a miracle for you, and he can't. Biroc's no better off than you are, wherever he is.'

Laszlo continued to stare for a moment, and then abruptly turned back to the broken fountain. He scooped his hand into the empty pool and raised it high. A pawful of fresh, sparkling water spattered down into the pool. Laszlo shook the paw dry. 'Details,' he said.

Romana searched for something to say. She was still searching when the Doctor called to them across the garden.

Laszlo didn't react at first; any voices that he heard, he assumed to be echoes from another time with no real presence in this one. But Romana recognised the Doctor immediately.

Laszlo glanced around when he saw Romana move, and then seemed to be worried by the figure that was crossing a stone piazza towards them.

'It's all right,' Romana reassured him, and then said to the Doctor as he arrived, 'How did you get here?'

'I'm still not sure about the details, but take a look at this.' He handed her K-9's memory wafer, supple and restored.

As she looked at it, the Doctor eyed the Tharil with interest.

'But this is a *new* memory wafer,' Romana said and then, looking up, added, 'Oh, and this is Laszlo. He helped me to escape from the slaver ship.'

'Pleased to—' the Doctor began, but broke off and said, 'Escape? Why were you even on the slaver ship?'

'It's a long story. I even managed to lose Adric and K-9.'

'Well, Rorvik's claws are out. If we're going to start pulling loose ends together we'll have to do it soon.'

'Biroc will know,' Laszlo said confidently.

'Sorry, Laszlo,' the Doctor said. 'I've seen Biroc, and he's no better off than we are.'

'But Biroc is our leader . . .'

'Biroc's been in chains, and he's been alone. It could take him a while to get his leadership skills back. Meanwhile, Tharils are dying.'

There was a long pause. Laszlo was still, as if restraining himself; but in the end he simply admitted, 'What you say is true.'

'Will you take us back to the mirrors? We can't do anything here.'

Laszlo hesitated, then nodded. He started to move away, and Romana hurried to catch up with him.

'I said the same things,' she whispered angrily. 'Why didn't you believe me?'

'The Doctor has authority. His words are to be accepted.'

'And why aren't mine?'

'You follow. The word of a follower is worth consideration but does not command obedience. That is the Tharil way.'

'I'm as qualified as he is.'

'But still you follow.'

It was true; and even though she wanted to say that it wasn't the whole story, she had no answer for him. She dropped back and found herself alongside the Doctor, an apprentice again.

The Doctor said, 'Any ideas about the Gateway?'

'Ideas?'

'Think of the nature of it. Interchanges between realities. Layers of space, and shadows of time.'

'Could it be linked to the CVE?'

'You tell me.'

Romana thought a moment longer, and then said excitedly, 'The Gateway *is* the CVE!'

'Like the TARDIS, a thing that has no set form of its own can take any.'

'So,' said Romana, 'this is the way back to our own universe, and . . . the way back to Gallifrey.' She paused. 'And then it's all going to end, isn't it?'

'I'd have thought you'd be pleased. The number of times you've been annoyed with me, the number of times you've complained. Telling me that I'm messing about without plans or purpose . . .'

'While I was looking for technical solutions. Easy to predict and easy to forestall.'

The Doctor smiled. 'Physics can only take you so far. The universe is an equation too vast to compute . . .'

'So, it's better to flow with it.'

'That's the way.'

She sniffed. 'Not the Time Lords' way.'

'Well, there's always an alternative.' The Doctor moved on to catch up with Laszlo.

Romana was left to think about those words. Unfortunately, they didn't alter the facts; when she got back to Gallifrey she'd resume her formal place in the Time Lord hierarchy. She'd be expected to behave with all the gravity and rationality that suited her position. There was no way of avoiding it. Unless . . .

The force of what the Doctor had been saying suddenly hit her.

She had to stop and take a deep breath before she could go on.

*

Rorvik stared into the mirror through which Biroc had originally disappeared. Nestor and Pieman Joe were leaning hard on their improvised crowbars, trying to prise out a block of masonry that formed part of an arch. But the stone didn't seem to have enough room to work its way out. Rorvik decided to give it some help.

He drew his pistol and put a couple of shots into the crack.

He didn't seem much bothered about one of his men getting in the way. Nestor dropped his crowbar on his own foot and limped away, howling. Rorvik gestured another crewman to take his place.

'Now, heave!' he said. 'I want to hear a few bones cracking!'

He left them to it and went back into the main hall.

Jos was waiting with the radio. 'Clearance on the interference, Captain!' he said.

'"Clearance on the interference!"' Rorvik mimicked and snatched the radio. 'Well?' he barked into it.

'Packard here.' The signal was poor.

'You're going to tell me that one of the Tharils got out.'

'Yes . . .'

'You're going to tell me there was a woman with him.'

'Yes, but . . .'

'You're going to tell me what she was doing on my ship,' Rorvik said, his voice rising to a shout, 'when *everybody knows it's bad luck to have a woman on board!*'

There was a pause, and then Packard said, 'You mean, things could get worse?'

'For you, it can be arranged. Who was she?'

'She just kind of . . . appeared. We think she's with the Doctor.'

'So you lost us a hostage.'

'It was you who lost us the Doctor.'

'Don't answer back.' Rorvik glanced into the alcove. The stone block had almost been worked free. Once it was out, the others should follow easily. 'Just hang around and you'll see some high-class leadership in action. We're going to bust open this ruin and drag everybody out by their tails.'

Over by the door, Nestor, who had a better view of the work, was starting to look worried.

Rorvik ignored him. 'Just stand by,' he told Packard. 'I'm going to check on the progress of the master plan.' He carried the radio over to the arch, and his satisfaction evaporated.

Where the stones had been levered out there was a large gap a couple of feet square; the mirror continued seamlessly behind the wall.

They could take out all the stone they wanted. Nothing was going to get them round the mirrors.

Rorvik's anger was now cold, restrained. 'Everybody get their gear together,' he said. 'Assemble by the main doorway and be ready to return to the ship.'

The crew started to move out.

Over the radio Packard said, 'What's the idea?'

'We're going to blast this gateway apart,' Rorvik said. '*That's* the idea. I should have done it straight off, but that's what I get for being the kind of man who exercises restraint.'

He tossed the radio to Jos and stalked through into the banqueting hall.

'Come on,' he shouted at the group around the table, 'Let's move it!'

Lane saw Packard sigh and rise to his feet behind the communications desk. Everyone was used to Rorvik's way of ending a conversation. No farewells, no signing off, he simply walked away. The man had the manners of a Thark.

Lane was by the rail with Sagan, the desk's usual occupier. Both had been watching Packard and trying to appear as if they weren't. Packard walked across the bridge towards them. He took his time, hands behind his back.

'Well?' he said as he came near. He sounded almost genial. 'Are you feeling good?'

The approach puzzled Lane. As a general handyman and dogsbody, he didn't have much experience of irony. He said, 'Should we be?'

'Maybe not, considering you let it all happen.'

'I don't see how we're to blame,' Sagan muttered, looking somewhere else.

'Somebody's got to stand up and take the mud, and

it isn't going to be me.' Packard looked hard at Sagan, and his manner lost much of its lightness. 'If Rorvik wants heads to dance on, I'll give him yours. Who left a fit Tharil for dead in the storeroom? And then couldn't stop him when he made a run for it?'

'Anybody would think . . .' Sagan began, but Packard was ignoring him and had turned to Lane.

'Who,' he went on, 'couldn't even manage to get in his way?'

'He was out of phase,' Lane tried to explain. 'Him and the woman. Nobody could lay a hand on them.'

Packard turned away. 'I'm not interested in your excuses.'

'Then why are you asking us?' Lane said, bewildered, and Sagan had to elbow him to shut him up.

Packard reached for the nearest microphone, and twisted it towards him on its flexible stalk. There was a ripping sound – the stalk had once been repaired with tape. Packard flicked the microphone's switch over to public address, and his amplified voice echoed from the bridge speakers.

'Now hear this,' he said, 'I'm saying this once and once only. Our beloved captain is on his way back.' Several crewmen – mostly the ones out of sight down the central well – booed half-heartedly. 'That's right, we all want to give him the welcome he deserves. But we're going to be nice to him, instead. Everybody to their positions as for a condition red emergency. For the moment I'll overlook the fact that when we had a condition red emergency, nobody seemed to know where they were supposed to be. Start feeding fuel into the sub-warp engines and get them up to full capacity.'

Lane raised a hand to catch Packard's attention. Packard turned an unsympathetic eye towards him.

'Remember what I was telling you about the missile strike,' Lane said. 'Nearly hitting the main power routings.'

'It didn't hit them?' Packard said coldly.

'Not quite.'

'So why are you telling me about it?'

Lane thought for a moment. How to frame the answer? But Packard wasn't interested – he'd already turned away to start checking on everyone's stations for the condition red. Crewmen were swapping seats and trading notes on little scraps of paper.

Sagan was nudging him in the ribs again and, when Lane looked round, the communications clerk jerked his head in the direction of the door.

The message was plain; *Let's get out of here until it's all blown over*.

Lane took another brief look at Packard's back, and then nodded briefly.

The two sidled off towards the bridge doors.

Packard didn't even look round as they made their escape.

*

In the fall of a coin was a tiny sample of the behaviour of its universe. Which continued to be lucky for Adric, since K-9 no longer seemed to be capable of helping with the navigation. After a while it had been impossible even to roll him as his drives locked solid.

So Adric got a grip on K-9's body case and lifted him, but the computer was heavy and the going was slow. It would have been even slower if Adric had checked his course more often, but he preferred to stagger on for as long as he could manage before setting the robot down. There was then the possibility that he could be heading for too long in the wrong direction.

Adric didn't own a timepiece. They weren't common on his own world, and since joining the Doctor he'd had no reason to acquire one; everywhere they went had a different length of day and of year, and each was divided differently for the convenience of the native civilisation.

And here, of course, there was no objective sense of time at all.

He eventually set K-9 down. His arms were quivering and he felt like he had no control over them. He'd have to rest for a moment.

As he recovered, he closed his eyes. He was aware of the danger in allowing himself to stare out into the void; it could be a soul-stealer if you let it. A few seconds of that white eternity, and your mind would slowly settle into a matching blankness and stay that way until something jogged you back – except, of course, being out here alone meant that there was nothing to jog you.

He pulled the token from his pocket. Still weakened, he could barely hold it. He flipped and then put out both hands to be sure of the catch.

It was several seconds before he realised that there was going to be no catch. He'd flipped the coin too hard, too high. The void had taken it.

His only means of navigation was lost.

'Do you think he knows where he's going?' the Doctor murmured to Romana. Laszlo seemed to be having trouble finding his way back to the section of the Gateway that projected into the void. He would stop at each junction in the castle, eyes narrowed and head cocked, to catch the faint sounds that drifted towards them. Sounds of celebration were the most frequent, but once there came a pitiful howling which turned Laszlo around in his tracks.

Laszlo's broad back was before them as he turned from one side to the other at a corridor intersection. They'd just walked down a long picture gallery that had no pictures, only squares in the dust where they'd hung.

'Well,' Romana said with ill-suppressed doubt, 'he *is* a Tharil . . .'

'Not a great recommendation, on their performance so far,' the Doctor rejoined. The story of Tharil greatness was one thing. Depending on such faded glory for survival was another. 'It's fair to say the situation's critical. Adric's lost, and K-9's failing.'

'Yes ... Where did you get the new memory wafer?'

'It wasn't new.'

'What?'

'It was one of the old ones. Passing through the mirror restored it. If we can bring K-9 through ...'

Laszlo was getting ahead of them.

'Don't lose sight of him,' Romana said with new determination.

I think, therefore I am. Adric remembered the phrase as an assertion that the Doctor liked to teach to computers. He'd said that it was essential to give a machine something to be proud of, otherwise it might brood too much and give you less than its best.

At this moment, the same phrase was Adric's hook on sanity.

He believed that he now understood the nature of the void – it had none. He'd been thinking of it as a kind of foggy planet-surface, where everything stood on its own piece of ground and kept up a relationship of space and distance with everything else, but it wasn't so. Relationships in the void only existed as long as they were seen to exist; turn your back, and everything drifted.

In his state of exhaustion, he'd made the mistake of

failing to watch the coin. And so, unobserved, it had been freed of the obligation to behave according to the rules and fall.

Now he knelt with his hand on the inert K-9, and looked around for any shape or outline that would re-establish his link with reality.

'The coin is nothing,' Biroc said.

The alien stood some way off, a silhouette blurred by the mists.

Hijacker or not, he was a welcome sight. Adric got to his feet and almost ran across to the Tharil, but then remembered K-9. If he were to turn his back, who could say if K-9 might still be there when next he looked.

Biroc repeated, 'The coin is nothing, no magic. The randomness is all. Remember.' And he started to walk away.

Adric should have shouted, but he simply watched Biroc go.

The coin is nothing? That seemed like open stupidity – with it he could move anywhere, without it he was lost.

And then he realised what Biroc meant.

The randomness is all. There was no magic in the fall of the coin.

All that mattered was the sample of the moment that it gave. But anything could be read as a sample. That was the very reason why the coin had been effective.

There was a blue star on his jacket, a badge that he'd always worn with pride.

He unpinned it and flipped it into the air, making sure that his eyes followed every stage of its spin. It dropped into his hand with the reverse side showing.

Perhaps Laszlo's senses were more acute than they seemed, or perhaps he was learning as he went along. In either case, he eventually got them back to the banqueting hall.

The Doctor's first passage through a mirror had been too sudden and unexpected for him to remember much about it. This time he didn't have the added distraction of rushing towards his own reflection and expecting a sharp crack on the head. As he stepped through the frame it felt like a line of coldness that washed across and through his body.

Romana was right behind him. 'Nobody home,' she said.

Some of the candles were still lit; others had burned right down and were only smouldering. Rorvik's men had left a heap of litter on and around the end of the table. The Doctor picked up a discarded wrapper and turned it over: *Snook's Yam Jelly, A Treat For Your Belly.* But then something else caught the Doctor's attention.

'Philistines!' he said as he stooped to pick something up. 'Barbarians!'

Romana said, 'You wouldn't expect Rorvik's men to clear up their mess, would you?'

'It's worse than that,' the Doctor said.

He'd found his scarf.

It was half-buried under the debris, and scraps were still clinging to it. As he knocked them away, he glanced down the table at Laszlo. The Tharil was by the fireplace, brooding over the debris of old carnage.

'Well, Laszlo,' the Doctor called, 'any idea what Rorvik's game might be?'

It was a moment before Laszlo showed any awareness that he was being spoken to and a moment longer before he came up with an answer. He shrugged and said, 'Something bad.'

'That goes without saying. I'd expected to find him trying to chisel his way through the walls.' And then something seemed to occur to the Doctor. 'What kind of weapons has he got?'

'Nothing significant.'

'Nothing at all?'

It seemed to cost Laszlo an effort to pull himself away from the fireplace. 'Nothing detectable,' he said. 'A slaver needs to be able to sneak past a civilised system without giving his secret away. Blatant weaponry would invite suspicion.'

'So, we can assume that they won't try to blast their way through,' the Doctor said.

Romana said, 'Why not try tossing a coin to find out?'

'Don't be ridiculous,' the Doctor told her, but she wasn't going to let him off so easily.

'It was your idea.'

'That was a philosophical exercise. Angels dancing on the head of a pin, and all that. I'd never suggest it would be reliable . . .'

At about the same time as the Doctor was denying the practicality of the system that he'd originally advocated, Adric was staggering into sight of the TARDIS. The distances for which he could carry K-9 were getting shorter, but as a result of that his course-checks became more frequent and his navigation more accurate.

If the Doctor had been able to show more faith in his own speculations, the events of the next hour might have been far less complicated.

Laszlo had wandered off again. To the Doctor, he seemed depressed, inattentive; he ran his hand along the panelling on a wall, as if trying to draw from it some of the former greatness of the Tharils.

A slave, the Doctor thought to himself; Laszlo's forgotten how to be anything else.

Now Laszlo was over by the entranceway. Rorvik's men had left the heavy doors open to the void, and

Laszlo looked out. The Doctor and Romana both saw his reaction at the same time, and they were with him even before he could turn and call.

The privateer was a dim, featureless bulk glimpsed through the fog. It was off the ground and turning slowly, putting its back and its massive engines towards the Gateway.

The Doctor said, 'They've got no weapons, no lasers?'

Laszlo didn't take his eyes from the privateer, his prison. 'None,' he said.

'So what can they be planning?'

The ship continued to turn. Now the thrust of the sub-warp lifting engines was carried towards them as a rumble almost too low to hear.

This is wrong, the Doctor thought; *they're too close.*

The Tharil suddenly growled in an agony of self-torment. 'Laszlo is blind,' he said. '*That* is their defence.'

'Running away?' Romana hazarded.

'Back in the days when there was a Tharil fleet, the slavers made secret visits to our system. They did not come openly, as they come today, dropping their nerve gases and collecting the fallen from the rock plains – they slipped in by the shadow of our moon. Our ships would pursue them, and the slavers developed the trick of overloading their engines to create a powerful backblast – it was more potent than any laser.'

The Doctor said, 'It looks like they're going to try it now.'

143

'What does he think will happen?' Romana said, and there was awe in her voice. Her mind had taken the short jump ahead to see the consequences of Rorvik's strategy.

'All the energy will be reflected straight back at them,' the Doctor realised, 'but obviously, Rorvik's too dim to grasp that. He'll destroy his own ship, the TARDIS, everything. Let's move.'

As they hurried down the short tunnel and out into the void, the rumble of the sub-warps grew louder.

The sound penetrated Adric's consciousness; or rather, his unconsciousness, as he was sprawling with his back to the TARDIS, too exhausted to raise the energy to get K-9 inside and hooked up to a power point. As he came blearily awake, he remembered what he was supposed to be doing; he rolled over painfully and managed to stagger to his feet. It was then that he became aware of the specific sound that had disturbed him.

As he stepped out of the shelter of the police box, high-speed winds took him by surprise and caught at his clothes and hair. He blinked back the wind-driven tears that were blinding him. On the far side of the TARDIS, the privateer ship had turned and was beginning to settle. It was frighteningly near; he should have seen it coming, but it threw no shadow.

And the TARDIS was squarely before the privateer's main engine.

'Go steady now, you crawlers,' Rorvik barked. It felt good to be in command of a ship again instead of a mobile picnic. 'I want a landing that wouldn't ripple the skin on a custard.'

The angle on the Gateway had been checked and confirmed, and the privateer began to settle in her new position. Packard counted aloud the seconds to touchdown.

There was a resounding boom throughout the ship and the bridge heaved violently; papers slid off desks and the loose head of a talkback microphone bounced across the floor.

Rorvik was quite pleased; as his crew's landings went, it wasn't bad. He clasped his hands behind his back and began to stride along the bridge. 'Status report from the helm,' he said grandly.

'What?' said Nestor, caught unawares.

'Status report.' Rorvik waited, but Nestor still obviously didn't understand. 'How is everything?'

'Fine, thanks,' said Nestor, still mystified.

Rorvik was starting to get impatient. 'Got any figures for me?'

Nestor hesitated. He looked at the mass of readouts that blinked all around the helm. He knew the meanings of no more than half of them. He said, 'Which ones would you like?'

Rorvik dismissed him with a gesture and moved on. 'Who's got control of the overload power?' he demanded. 'Anybody?'

'I think it's me,' came a small voice from the other side of the bridge. It was Jos.

'I thought it was me,' said Dulles, who had returned to his post.

Rorvik sighed loudly, so everyone could hear. 'Anyone else want to put in a bid? Anyone got half an idea of what's supposed to be happening here?' One or two hands went up, but he ignored them. 'Just as a point of information, we're going to be handling an overload that could blow us into scrambled Thark eggs, and I'd appreciate it if the odd one or two of you could make a small effort and pay some attention to the work.'

Most of Dulles's attention was on the monitor screen in front of him. 'Hey,' he whispered to the man at the next position, 'you know that little blue box thing? It's in the way.'

'Yeah,' the other said happily. 'Let's see how far we can blow it.'

It didn't take any time at all to cross from the Gateway to the TARDIS.

Distances within the void were now shrinking

perceptibly, the major masses that had created a mini-universe between them now drawing closer together. The Doctor even thought of a neat analogy that could be used to demonstrate the principle in a Gallifreyan masterclass; the void as a featureless sheet of rubber, the separate masses placed on it in the form of weighted globes – only to roll together towards a common centre, where perhaps their combined weight would tear through the sheet and take them to ... where?

A neat analogy, and a shame it would never be used. Not that the Doctor was unduly pessimistic about their situation, serious though it was. It was simply that no one had ever asked him to conduct a masterclass.

They found Adric trying to manhandle K-9 over the threshold and into the TARDIS.

'You found your way back, then?' the Doctor said.

'K-9 doesn't respond—' Adric began urgently, but the Doctor cut him short.

'Marvel as, with a flourish, I produce the answer to all his ...'

The exposition tailed off as the memory wafer crumbled in his fingers.

A few seconds, and it was dust. No answer at all.

He compared the deterioration of the wafer with his own hand, which remained whole; the inert matter temporarily restored, but the living matter permanently renewed.

But they had no time to waste. With Laszlo following, Romana gave Adric a hand to get K-9 inside while the Doctor went straight to the console and began preliminary checks for a dematerialisation. Laszlo stood back a little way and watched him. He didn't marvel at the incongruous relative proportions of the ship as most newcomers did; the Doctor supposed that any being with the Gateway in its history would probably take such wonders calmly.

'We have to get out of the way before the fireworks start,' the Doctor explained. His idea had been to make a blind leap through the Gateway and then have the TARDIS establish coordinates – any coordinates – in the N-Space universe on the other side, their home reality. Now Rorvik's rash plan was threatening to ruin all that, and perhaps even close off the Gateway for ever.

'"Out of the way"?' Laszlo said. 'Where?'

'Doesn't really matter at the moment, does it? Anywhere's better than squarely behind the main engine.'

'And Laszlo's people,' the Tharil said, 'down there in the hold? What of them when the backblast comes?'

Even though time was limited, the Doctor broke off to explain with tact and patience. 'Laszlo, there's nothing we can do. If I could get in and stop them, I would. But it's too late for that.'

'Biroc would know what to do,' Laszlo said stubbornly, and the Doctor began to get annoyed.

'Well,' he said, 'it's a pity he isn't here.'

'I know a way in,' said Adric at his elbow.

The Doctor ignored the boy. 'We'd either have to take the bridge by force, which would be difficult for all three and a half of us, or else we'd have to sabotage the engines ...'

Adric said, 'I know how to do that, too.'

'... and I don't think you can have much idea of how complicated a Minados warp system is.' He frowned as Adric's words worked their way through. 'What are you talking about?'

'There's a hole in the side of the ship where the missile hit them,' Adric explained. 'You can climb in easily. And then, when I was listening at the door, I heard one of the crewmen talking. He said something about the main ... the main power something being uncovered.'

Romana had finished the hook-up and now joined them. 'He's right about the hole,' she said. 'The rest I wouldn't know.'

The Doctor held up a hand for silence and began to concentrate for a moment. If the power lines were uncovered ... and if they could be reached ... and if they carried the power to and from the bridge controls ...

Romana said, 'What are we waiting for?'

'You're waiting for me and Laszlo to get back.'

'But I ...'

149

He stopped her with a slight nod towards Adric, and of course she couldn't argue; if the plan somehow failed, he couldn't be left to burn in the backblast. Adric was about to speak, and the Doctor said, 'Before you ask, the answer's no.'

'You don't even know the question,' Adric protested.

'Don't I? You're staying here with Romana, and she's going to hit the go button if anything goes wrong. Come on, Laszlo.'

And without further arguments, the Doctor and the Tharil ran for the door.

WARP SYSTEMS ON HALF-POWER AND HOLDING
OVERLOAD SYSTEMS PRIMED AND HOLDING
MECHANICAL ESTIMATES — UNAVAILABLE
TARGET ESTIMATES — MANUAL CONTROL
DESTINATION COORDINATES — MANUAL CONTROL
FAILSAFE CUTOUTS — RE-ENGAGED

REMINDER: THE THIRD INSTALMENT PAYMENTS ON
THE MOBIUS GENERATOR ARE NOW DUE

REC ROOM COFFEE DISPENSER REMAINS INOPERABLE
REC ROOM SAUNA INOPERABLE
REC ROOM 3V INOPERABLE
REC ROOM MASSAGE UNIT INOPERABLE
REC ROOM CORRIDOR — LIGHTS FAILURE IMMINENT
SEE 01/00/2223 FOR SYSTEMS CHECK

Rorvik was looking over Dulles's shoulder, his initial businesslike enthusiasm deteriorating into weariness. The young crewman's method of operation was, to put it kindly, experimental .

'No,' Rorvik said as Dulles reached for an obsolete control that was connected to nothing at all. 'Try something else.' All over the rest of the bridge, his crewmen were conversing in puzzled groups as they tried to work out the functions of systems they'd never used before.

The bridge doors slid open. 'Bins!' Waldo shouted as he entered.

'Let's 'ave your bins!' Aldo joined in from just behind. 'We 'aven't got all day.'

The attention-grabbing impact of Rorvik's shout was only slightly less than that of an erupting volcano. 'If those two old buzzards aren't off my bridge in ten seconds, tell them they'll be carrying their teeth around in a little paper bag!'

There was a sudden silence. Everyone stared at Aldo and Waldo.

Waldo said, 'Well, if you—'

'Out!'

The two of them were gone from the bridge in a second.

As the doors closed behind them, Dulles finished flicking a sequence of switches and allowed himself a small moment of satisfaction.

'There,' he said, and Rorvik turned back to take a look.

At first, he said nothing. Then he slapped Dulles on the shoulder, as if in confirmation of success. 'Congratulations,' he said. 'You just opened the loading bay doors. If we were in space right now, we'd all be dead. Keep up the good work.'

He moved on, leaving Dulles to look crestfallen, and came level with two empty seats. He looked at them.

'This is great,' he said. 'I'm having one of the worst days of my life and now half my crew go missing. Where are Sagan and Lane?'

Sagan and Lane were looking for some quiet corner of the ship where they could play a few hands of cards and ride out the worst of Rorvik's temper. Normally that would have meant the crew recreation room, but they'd found the floor and the outer corridor awash; the coffee spigot had been leaking and left unattended, and most of the underfloor wiring was starting to short out. So, they decided to head for the storage holds instead, where they could push a few boxes together and make the place a little more like home.

The loading bay door was opening onto the void as they passed through, the result of Dulles's mistake. It stopped as it was three-quarters of the way open, and then abruptly started to lower again. The two crewmen walked on past, as if they'd seen it all before and expected nothing better.

Which was how they missed seeing Biroc as he stepped through the gap and melted into the shadows of the loading bay.

Meanwhile, the Doctor and Lazlo had entered through the one breach in the ship's outer skin that Rorvik couldn't expect to seal.

'Well?' Laszlo said impatiently. 'Begin.'

The Doctor was looking over the maze of wiring and conduit that was the privateer's warp control system. He said, 'I can't.' Laszlo took a threatening step towards him, and he added, 'I've never seen anything like this before.'

'You said they were Minados.'

'That bit's Minados,' the Doctor said, pointing. 'And so's that. This is a Trevillian coupler which shouldn't even be in a warp engine, that looks like part of a Fulton stabiliser … it's the most incredible lash-up I've ever seen. This could take hours.'

'We have minutes.'

'Then we'd better find some way of getting to the bridge and stopping Rorvik.'

It was at that moment they heard the locking bolts slam home in the airlock overhead. They climbed alongside the machinery to the catwalk; powerful

Laszlo made it first and reached back to give the Doctor a hand.

The points of his claws brushed the Doctor's wrist as he felt himself lifted. It was probably an accident – but it might have been a reminder.

The Doctor gave the airlock a critical onceover. It was built for pressure and so couldn't easily be forced, even with Laszlo's strength. But perhaps there was another way; there was a small panel on the frame with a touch-open button and an emergency pressure sensor. If pressure in the compartment dropped and the airlock was open for some reason, the sensor would automatically close it without need of command. But that could leave engineers trapped inside; if the emergency conditions subsided, there had to be some way to let the trapped personnel escape.

There was a red light over the panel. Actually, it was an ordinary white light under a red plastic screw-on dome, and the Doctor removed this. He placed it over the sensor and pressed down tight, covering it with both hands.

Laszlo was looking puzzled.

'When the air under here gets warm,' the Doctor explained, 'the pressure goes up. If the door's got an independent all-clear circuit, we might be able to trip it.'

The theory sounded good. He only hoped it would work in practice.

*

'Saw Aldo and Waldo earlier,' Lane said.

Sagan was studying his cards and frowning. It was a good hand, but he didn't want Lane to think so. He said, 'Oh, yes?'

'Got me wondering. You always see them moving rubbish around. Never actually see where it goes.'

'Goes?'

Lane looked at his cards and sighed. It was a good hand, but he didn't want Sagan to think so. 'In the end,' he said. 'We only ever see it moving from one place to another.'

'That's all it does. Why don't we dump it into space?'

'Unhygienic.'

Sagan was first to hear the outer airlock door sliding open. He and Lane had several seconds before the cycle could be completed for the inner door, only a few feet away from them, to open in turn. They wasted part of the time looking from the airlock to each other and back again, and Sagan also managed to sneak a look at the cards Lane was holding. But when Laszlo and the Doctor came through, both crewmen were on their feet with sidearms drawn.

'Ah,' said the Doctor, as if he'd suddenly remembered a complication that could alter the running of whatever he was up to.

'Don't move,' Sagan said.

'No one's actually moving,' the Doctor said.

Sagan had them both put their hands on their heads.

He made a point of staying well out of Laszlo's reach; he'd never again make the mistake of being casual in his handling of Tharils. The only time a Tharil was safe was when he was sleeping like a stone and living out of a bunch of tubes, or else in chains. Well, Rorvik had wanted a live Tharil for a navigator, and now he could have one. He'd also wanted the Doctor; he was going to get quite a package.

The Doctor and Laszlo were marched out of the storage complex by Sagan and Lane, through the loading bay. It was in the corridors beyond this, making their way towards the main bridge access way, that the Doctor glimpsed Biroc.

Nobody else saw the Tharil, not even Laszlo. It was almost as if Biroc had shown himself to the Doctor for some specific reason and then withdrawn. But why? The bridge wasn't far ahead; the privateer was primed and almost ready for the backblast that would destroy the Gateway, the slave ship and possibly even the TARDIS itself.

They came to the rec room corridor. There were no lights, and the floor seemed to be awash with thick, treacly liquid. The whole party slowed, and Lane gave the Doctor a prod in the back with his pistol.

The Doctor said, 'Rather dark, isn't it?'

'What's the matter,' said Lane, 'you want somebody to hold your hand?'

The Doctor froze. Then he smiled appreciatively. 'What a splendid idea!'

Fortunately, Laszlo had picked up on the same notion. As their hands touched, they slid out of phase together.

Each threw out a free arm, and Sagan and Lane were both slammed back against the corridor walls.

Before Sagan could warn him, Lane tried to get off a shot at the two retreating figures. The charge hit the outer rim of the aura and bounced back at him, zapping and zigzagging from wall to wall; in an attempt to dodge the ricochets, both he and Sagan ended up on the corridor floor covering their heads.

'Rorvik isn't going to like us,' Lane said as his shot zipped by overhead and finally petered out in a rain of sparks from the ceiling.

'He doesn't like us anyway,' Sagan replied. 'Just tell him.'

Lane got to his feet and went over to the nearest intercom point. The wall around it was scorched and smouldering. He tapped in the captain's code and heard, a couple of moments later, Rorvik's voice in response, 'Bridge.'

How to explain? This was the second time they'd both managed to lose Laszlo, and there was no obvious way of making it look good. He began, 'Ah . . . I thought I'd better warn you, Captain . . . You'll be getting a couple of visitors any time now . . .'

Sagan glanced heavenward and turned away.

Rorvik never heard the rest of the message. He slammed his fist down on the intercom button to shut it off. '"A couple of visitors"?' he echoed, his face thunderous. 'That's it, that's enough. I've warned Aldo and Waldo, they don't set foot on this bridge again.'

He stalked across the bridge to the sliding doors, yelling as he went. The crew shrank back nervously as he passed. 'As soon as we get back into normal space, I'm stuffing them into their own waste bag and shoving them out of the nearest airlock.'

There was a metal handle set into the wall by the doors; he grasped it and gave it a quarter-turn. A sign illuminated in a panel above it: EMERGENCY DOOR SEAL ACTIVATED. Then he thumbed the button on the ever-present intercom alongside. 'Aldo and Waldo, are you listening to me? From now on you stay off this bridge unless you've got specific permission and even *then* you'd better be sure that I'm not around when you arrive ...'

Aldo and Waldo were nowhere in earshot; in fact, at that moment they were in a stateroom that they'd found and cleared out for their own use a long time before Rorvik had ever even considered his chances of a captaincy. It was the Doctor and Laszlo who arrived outside the bridge, out of phase, and slid back into normality in time to hear Rorvik's voice raving out of the door intercom at the empty air.

'. . . *you haven't got the remotest idea of what the pressures are like in an operational area and what's more, you don't seem to care. If there was any higher authority than me on board, I'd report you to him, so consider yourselves lucky you've got such a kind-hearted and tolerant captain and not somebody of average sensibilities who'd no doubt consign you to the horrible fate you so richly deserve . . .'*

The Doctor said to Laszlo, 'I think we're locked out. Can you pass us through?'

'This door is too dense,' Laszlo said.

Suddenly the Doctor understood. He placed his hand against the door. The structure, the skin of the ship – it had to be dwarf star alloy. A dwarf star was formed when a sun burned itself out and collapsed. The material compressed under its own weight, reaching a density that couldn't be achieved by any industrial process. Techniques had, however, been developed to make use of some of the material's properties in an alloy.

It explained so much. The manacles that anchored the time-sensitives to a single reality. The powerful engines, far out of proportion to the size of the ship. The very shrinking of the void, as the sheer mass of the dwarf star alloy caused their mini-cosmos to collapse in on itself.

'There isn't much choice,' the Doctor said. 'It's pull the power lines or nothing.'

And since the jerry-rigged mess that was supposed to be a Minados warp control system was completely unfamiliar to the Doctor, he had a fear that it would probably be nothing.

'. . . and see how you like *that*!' Rorvik knocked off the intercom switch with some satisfaction and turned to survey the rest of the bridge. Nobody was working, and everybody was looking at him. His expression started to darken again.

'What's this, a free show? Get the ship ready for the overload.'

Packard cleared his throat. 'It *is* ready,' he said.

'Oh,' Rorvik said, slightly thrown. 'Right. Start the power build.'

Packard pulled one of the flexible microphones towards him. When he spoke, his voice would be heard throughout the privateer.

'Attention all zones,' he said. 'We are building to a deliberate tactical overload. Expect the blast when we reach one hundred and five . . .'

'. . . *present level is seventy-three and building.*'

'Seventy-three,' the Doctor said gravely as they let themselves through the air lock and back into the warp control compartment.

'What does it mean?' Laszlo said.

'Haven't got a clue.'

They hurried across the catwalk and began to climb down towards the damaged section.

The Doctor said, 'Any idea what you're looking for?'

'No.'

'Well, that makes two of us. I'd suggest we split the whole thing, take a different area each.'

'. . . *Eighty-five and building* . . .'

The Doctor was thinking. The situation was grave. The reflected energy of a backblast would be devastating, and only something like a TARDIS in transit had a chance of evading it. Should that be the case, Romana and Adric would be safe; if he failed here, she could be relied upon to make the hard choice. Biroc had thrown away his own chances by making a return to the privateer. And for what? To die with his fellow-slaves?

'. . . *Ninety-two and building* . . .'

Laszlo surveyed his section of the control circuits with a sense of impotence; Tharils were intuitive, they knew nothing of engineering. He could be looking straight at the lines that they needed to disconnect, and he wouldn't even know it.

But then he saw Lane's clipboard.

He had to pull himself up to be level with it. The damage control forms had been pushed in behind some fat snakes of cable to hold them in place; this had obviously happened since the missile hit – in which case, surely this was the area where he needed to be.

'. . . *Ninety-eight and building . . .*'

The Doctor was beginning to realise that his choice was a mistake. The Trevillian coupler occupied most of this area, and none of that had even been touched by the damage.

He thought darkly of Biroc, whose invasion of the TARDIS had sparked the chain of events pitching to this present crisis. But no, he realised, to blame Biroc was ungenerous; the fault lay in slavery. Biroc had only done the best he could in trying to escape.

But might not Biroc be safe whatever happened? A storm of time winds would be raised by the backblast, but Biroc could probably just slide out of phase and ride the holocaust until it subsided. So could Laszlo, for that matter, or any Tharil who was sufficiently conscious to make use of his ability to cut himself loose from the moment.

Now, there was the basis of a plan, even if it was too late to do anything about it. If only Biroc could have looked into the future, could have seen the pattern of events that lay ahead as he ran from the privateer to ride the time winds and seek out the TARDIS . . . But then, wasn't that what Tharils did? Wasn't it that skill that made them so valuable?

Of course it was.

*

'. . . *One hundred even. Stand by for overload.*'

As understanding was dawning for the Doctor, Laszlo was feeling his excitement rise. *These must the cables*, he thought, *and if they aren't then what do I have to lose?*

There was a growing rumble from deep inside the ship, and the floor below was starting to vibrate. He thrust a paw under the main power lines and tensed himself ready to rip them all out in a single heave.

'*One hundred and five, we have overload.*'

The rumble became a roar, the vibration an earthquake.

And then the Doctor's hands closed on Laszlo's ears, pulling the Tharil's head back.

'Stop!' the Doctor shouted.

Laszlo howled, more in anger than in pain, and he released the cables to push the Doctor away. When he turned back, he re-established his grip and pulled with all his considerable strength, At first nothing, and then with a rip they came away from the wall and were yanked free of the connection box above. Something went with a bang, and sparks fell like rain.

It was too late; the overload had begun, and nothing could stop it now.

But there was time for one little revenge. Laszlo turned on the Doctor. The one who had damned the imprisoned Tharils, when they might have been saved, could spend his last moments as unpleasantly as possible.

'Believe me, Laszlo, this overload is the only way,' the Doctor yelled, barely audible over the below-decks vibration of the warp motors.

The Tharil held out his paw and unsheathed his claws; fully extended, they were almost an inch long. The Doctor backed off, down towards the void fog and the torn metal of the privateer's side.

'This is what Biroc expected all along!'

It was the name that stopped Laszlo. And as the warp motors continued on their one-way climb to Armageddon, he stayed his hand and waited for whatever the Doctor was trying to say.

'Biroc knew that this would happen!' the Doctor shouted. 'He wanted it to happen, and that's why he waited and did nothing! The blast won't harm your people, It's part of his plan to *free* them!'

Biroc, meanwhile, was about halfway through his work. He'd made his way through the slave hold, briefly touching each of the sleeping forms that he passed and pushing them gently out of phase. Some of the younger and tougher Tharils were awake and alert already; they needed nothing to be explained to them but immediately started to disconnect themselves from the now-useless life supports. They moved through to the other levels of the hold, each touching more Tharils; the glow rippled through the darkened chambers like wildfire.

Each Tharil that came round was immediately presented with overlapping visions of only two possible futures: holocaust or survival. It was rare to be given such a clear-cut choice; the range of potential tomorrows was usually endless, with the least probable versions being the most difficult to perceive.

Which made Biroc's achievement as he'd lain in his shackles on the privateer's bridge all the more remarkable.

As the Doctor was now trying to explain to Laszlo, Biroc had managed to glimpse as a unity the events that would follow if the privateer and the TARDIS were to be brought together at the Gateway. There had been no randomness in his actions, and no indecisions in his failures to act.

When Biroc watched and did nothing, it was because he already knew what lay ahead.

As a piece of complex visualisation, it was fated to become Tharil legend; it wasn't for nothing that they called Biroc their leader.

Now even the older Tharils were shaking off the effects of the drugs and coming round. All were fit and clear-headed – the slavers, walking in alloy-plated armour and respirators across the alien plain as the nerve gases drifted around them, had picked only the best.

165

The last Tharil slipped into safety as the build-up in the warp motors finally reached critical.

Then the privateer exploded.

Romana had waited as long as she dared, and then a little longer.

But when the danger signals on the TARDIS console stopped flashing and became steady, she knew that it was too late to hope. Even then she might have delayed a moment longer, but a glance towards Adric reminded her that there were other responsibilities she had to acknowledge.

She operated the control to dematerialise.

There hadn't been time to attempt anything more sophisticated than a simple jump two or three minutes into the future. Such jumps weren't really practical as they took two or three minutes to effect and the saving in temporal terms was nil, but in the time that the trip was being processed they would be beyond the reach of the physical forces of their environment, and that was exactly what they needed.

For a moment, it looked as if she'd left it too late. The control room began to shiver as the blast of the slaver ship's engines washed across the spot where they'd been, but it was no more than an echo that they carried with them, and it had no true destructive force.

Romana watched the instruments on the console, searching them for clues to what might be happening outside. She saw masses move and change, energies flow, bursts of radiation; she observed the consequences of Rorvik's bull-headed and uninformed decision. It was much more than a simple backblast; it had brought about the total collapse of the small universe that had been formed in the void.

They'd all known that this pocket dimension was unstable, that the masses of the privateer and the TARDIS and the Gateway had been drawing themselves together towards an eventual collapse. Even the privateer's computer must have sensed the compression of mass that had made the ship measurably smaller. But Romana didn't suppose that Rorvik was in the habit of paying much attention to his computer, nor to anything else – not even when the distance from the privateer to the Gateway appeared to diminish each time it was crossed.

Matter is only energy locked down tight; energy is matter set free. As the privateer's warp motors released vast amounts of energy into the void, the collapse began to accelerate.

And the Doctor was somewhere out there, unprotected in the middle of it. He didn't have a chance.

Romana sighed and lowered her head. Adric was sitting by K-9 and holding on to the mobile computer for comfort. The charge lead linked K-9 to the wall socket, and Romana had wired in two of the static charge blocks but, apart from a weak glow of his operational lights to indicate that power was making its way through, there had been no response from him.

Adric said, 'What now?'

'Now?' Romana looked again at the console readouts. The matter of the void was being squeezed down a whirlpool. Lectures in temporal mechanics had taught her that reality, though infinitely flexible, was ultimately indestructible. The privateer would be spewed out somewhere, dismantled and dispersed and beyond recognition.

But Adric had asked her a question.

'Now?' she repeated. 'Nothing.'

The control room was suddenly flooded with a blinding light, so bright that she had to cover her eyes before she'd had a chance to see why. But she knew why; the doors were opening again.

Adric managed to peep out between his fingers. Everything outside was moving with dragging slowness, a sign that the TARDIS was still in transit; it seemed that the void itself was on fire, and pieces of the slaver ship were aflame as they were blasted around. Even the huge stones of the Gateway castle were burning, and one of the great wooden doors went spinning by and narrowly missed slamming its way through into the control room.

Romana seemed to have forgotten the pain of the light; she was rising from behind the console.

She'd seen that the Doctor and Laszlo were running for the TARDIS.

Their hands were linked and they were both out of phase, riding out the worst of the explosion. It was no easy run. The whirlpool forces dragged at them, and for some of the way they were actually losing more ground than they made.

It was Laszlo's strength that decided the matter, for when the Doctor was momentarily lifted off his feet and drawn back it was Laszlo who stood his ground and anchored him.

The second Gateway door sailed past close over-head, an airborne raft of fire. The Doctor and the Tharil ducked before making the effort to sprint the final distance to the waiting TARDIS.

Laszlo didn't cross the threshold. He handed the Doctor in and they parted, one inside and one outside.

The Doctor quickly stabilised into phase and the doors began to close behind him.

'Screen!' he shouted to Romana, as they lost their view of the disintegrating world outside. He held his shoulder as he moved across to the console; for some of the distance he'd bobbed like a puppet with only Laszlo's iron grip on his wrist to keep him down. His arm would ache for days, but he wouldn't mind. It would remind him that he was alive.

The screen opened to give them an exterior view.

The privateer had been stripped down to a skeletal wreck like the rotted corpse of a beached whale. But there was movement within it; Biroc was leading out a line of Tharils. They were free. But after all the destruction, where could they go?

The ribs of the privateer began to crumble. The reaction was burning itself out. As the scene began to clear a little more, Romana pointed: the Tharils' destination.

The stonework of the Gateway had been completely stripped away. There was no more banqueting hall with its thousand-year-old mouldering feast, and no ensemble of ghosts would ever play from the minstrels' gallery again.

But the mirrors were still there, untouched and unharmed, a black and glittering Stonehenge of wafers.

Biroc was the first to a mirror. His hand stretched out, and his aura melted into the surface. He stepped through, and the line followed. Tharil, after Tharil, after Tharil, after Tharil.

The void had one more surprise.

The privateer collapsed in on itself, driving the crew out of their shelter. It seemed impossible that they could have survived; and in truth, they hadn't. Yet some shadow of them still existed, wrenched from their timeline by forces reflected back from the Gateway. As they came stumbling out of the remains of their ship, they were ghostly and almost transparent. Rorvik was shouting but making no sound. All of them were blackened and smoking from the blast that had hurled them into this disjointed state. Aldo and Waldo were dragging a ghostly garbage bag with a hole torn in the bottom – spreading the rubbish into the Great Beyond.

Laszlo was the last to the Gateway. He lagged some distance behind, and as a figure re-emerged from the mirror it seemed as though one of the Tharils might have been sent back to check for him.

But it was no Tharil that stepped through.

It was one of the Gundan, armed and ready.

Laszlo hesitated, his escape route blocked. The mass murder that had begun on that spot an age before seemed about to be continued.

And what of the others that had passed through before him? Had the Gundan simply waited on the other side of the mirror, his victims obediently walking under the axe one at a time?

It is difficult to imagine the workings of the Gundan's dark soul. For an age it had waited, obedient to its prime command: to kill the brutes who rule. In some ways it was an uncomplicated creature, bent to a single purpose, but in order to operate independently in territory where its masters could never go it needed a measure of analytical judgement. Not much – never enough to allow it to reflect on its orders – just enough to let it carry them out. To seek out and punish the brutes who ruled.

And who were the rulers now? Who wore the chains, and who held the whips? Who ran, and who chased?

The Gundan had pondered these issues as it walked alone through the abandoned Gateway.

Now it walked on past Laszlo, ignoring him.

Its attention was on the crew of the privateer.

Rorvik saw it first. He saw it raise a three-fingered hand and make a beckoning motion.

Whereupon Rorvik swallowed, hard.

For the Doctor and Romana, considering how close they'd come to being wiped out, any ending could be considered happy if they lived to enjoy it. But there was one reservation, a shadow in the brightness of their relief.

K-9 had, it seemed, deteriorated beyond rescue.

In a way, it was ridiculous. A machine, a mobile computer; the thing had been built and could, if necessary, be built again. But once extinguished there was no way of reproducing its personality with any exactness; too many small and unpredictable factors were at work, and a copy would never be any more than just that. And, like anything with a personality, K-9 had become something other than a mere piece of the TARDIS's furniture.

He was still whole, but he was a relic. Everything was there, but none of it worked. Even the comparative alertness that he'd shown over recent hours had only lasted for as long as he could hold a charge; and when the power ran out, so did life.

'He'd be restored on the other side of the mirrors,' Romana said.

The Doctor shook his head. 'Restoration via the mirrors is a one-way trip, unless you're a biological system able to follow the pattern of the change on the return journey.' He held up his healed hand. 'You remember the state of the memory wafers I brought back with me. And if K-9 were to be put through and then abandoned, he'd be trapped and alone. It's no answer.'

'Give him to me, instead.'

'To you?'

Romana nodded. 'I'm not coming back with you, Doctor. It's time to choose, and this is the choice I'm making.'

The Doctor stared.

'You want to stay here?' Adric said, puzzled. 'Why? What will you do?'

'What the Doctor and I have always done.'

'With no TARDIS?' the Doctor reminded her.

'I don't need a TARDIS. I'll have the Gateway. I'll learn to use it the way Biroc's people used to.'

'You mean when they were the most vicious slavers in the known universe?'

She'd obviously thought it all out. 'There's my first job. Making sure history doesn't repeat itself.'

'Well . . .' That was it, then, the Doctor thought. It seemed that Romana's apprenticeship was, indeed, finally over. He'd known that it would be goodbye soon in any case; the Time Lords were expecting the return of one of their own. Now they'd be disappointed.

The Doctor started to smile, and it turned into a broad grin. Time Lords. They thought they knew how the whole universe ticked, and they considered themselves perfectly suited to supervise it. Such arrogance had always made him uncomfortable – which was why, many adventures before, he'd stolen the TARDIS and run, determined not to stay among their ranks. Now it seemed the message was starting to spread.

He said, 'I can only wish you good luck. It's not likely we'll meet again.'

'I know,' Romana said.

'Not impossible,' he added.

'Just improbable.'

'Quite,' the Doctor said. 'So let's just make it *au revoir*.'

For the Doctor and Adric, leaving the void would be a relatively simple matter; as with most problems, the main obstruction had been a lack of useful information.

Once it was known that the Gateway was actually formed from the fabric of the CVE – the Charged Vacuum Emboitement, a hole in space similar to that through which they'd originally fallen – then he had a target, the one essential they'd lacked in their earlier attempts to leave E-Space.

So the Doctor set the TARDIS a problem in theory: to forget for a while the existence of a larger universe, and to consider that the TARDIS and the circle of mirrors were everything. It took only minutes for the TARDIS to produce a mathematical summary of that mini-universe, and even less time for the Doctor to invert it. The coordinates, derived from that inversion and fed into the console, would put the TARDIS on the other side of the mirrors, and back into N-Space. From there he could pick their destination.

Simple, really. Simpler than so many things.

'Will Romana be all right, do you think?' Adric said.

'All right?' The Doctor turned to look at him sternly. His expression softened. 'She'll be superb.'

Romana sat on the mossy stone of the fountain in the hidden garden. Now a little water was spattering from the vents – real water, not just sounds. It showered into the bowl but didn't collect; the stone was cracked, and the water bled away into the ground beneath. But somewhere else in the garden the fountain was whole, and the water ran fresh; and somewhere even further away there was bare rich ground, as yet untouched by the ancient builders.

She'd chosen the spot well; no flip of the coin, but a good guess instead. Before her was a terrace, and then a shallow flight of steps led to a formal lawn. The maze was beyond this, hopelessly overgrown.

She didn't have to wait for long.

The sound was faint at first, but it quickly grew. It was an unmusical sound, a warning hoot; and as it grew louder a blue, double-cube shape, the form of an old Earth police box, slowly materialised in the middle of the lawn. It never reached full solidity but began instead to fade again, the gardens only a stepping-stone to new sights, new adventures.

Romana stayed for a while longer, watching the place where it had been. The grass, only briefly pressed down by its appearance, soon lost the marks of the materialisation. She became aware that somebody had moved in close beside her, but she knew who it was, and she was unworried.

'Regrets?' Laszlo said.

She took a breath, and then a last look. It was her farewell to the old life. 'Of course,' she said. 'But nothing would hold me back.'

Laszlo inclined his head to show his understanding, and the two of them walked across the terrace and away from the fountain.

K-9 stayed a little longer; his sensors were more acute, and the traces of the TARDIS took longer to fade.

But after a while he wheeled round and started down the path behind the Tharil and his mistress.

THE KAIROS RING

Romana stood among fallen stones on a grassy plain and thought, *Too late. At least a thousand years too late.*

The sky was stacked heavy with clouds, and dark. The big stones were rough-hewn and their placement made an almost perfect circle, but any ritual significance they'd had was long forgotten.

She was disappointed, mostly with herself. At this stage it was hard to say whether her information was wrong, or her instincts at fault. Either way, she'd brought them to a fruitless spot.

But then she saw something.

Romana dropped to one knee for a closer look, and then reached down to tug at the angle of metal she could see sticking out of the hard dirt. The dirt broke up, and a buckle came free. As she continued to pull, she drew a fragment of rotted leather strap out of the earth.

The buckle was D-shaped, and cast in the form of two bronze dolphins meeting head-to-head. It was lightly crusted, and discoloured green from its time in the ground. Late Roman, she reckoned, part of some soldier's armour, and the straight edge of the leather suggested that it had been cut with a blade. She even began to imagine that the dark stains on the strap might be blood.

Perhaps that was taking it too far, but one thing was for sure. The stones might be ancient but the battle was more recent, which meant that her timing was not as far out as she'd thought.

Under Laszlo's instruction, Romana was becoming more adept at navigating the Tharils' Gateway and taking advantage of the time winds. Even so, she was no Tharil herself. Such skills were not part of her nature, so they had to be acquired. It was no easy matter. Compared to travel within the protection of a TARDIS, riding the time winds was like free diving in a hostile ocean. Romana still couldn't slide out of phase unaided, and still couldn't reach a destination with sufficient accuracy.

But she was learning, and she was getting better.

She rose to her feet. Around her the grass rippled, and for a moment the clouds seemed to move at a greater speed. Even before she turned, she knew that Laszlo had joined her.

She showed him the buckle. 'I was close,' she said.

He didn't even look at the offered trinket. 'The Sluagh are on the move,' he said.

'Here?'

'Another battlefield.'

He held out his hand. It was like an enormous golden paw, fully in keeping with the leonine head and mane that sat above those broad shoulders. The Tharil cut a mighty figure, intimidating to all, but his touch was delicate, their contact slight as Romana let the buckle fall and took the offered hand.

Straight away she felt herself sliding out of phase with the moment, cutting loose from any fixed location of time or place. They'd come seeking the Sluagh, but the Sluagh were elsewhere. They'd leapt on ahead to another line of time, in another universe of possibilities. So the chase would continue, with Romana and the Tharil a step behind, sometimes getting closer, often losing the trail.

With the shifting of time came the ghosts; for a moment the old battle shimmered all around them, while beyond that, the early stones began to rise from where they'd fallen.

But Laszlo and Romana did not dwell upon the spectacle. They had somewhere more pressing to be.

Another time, another place, another battlefield. A battlefield of the American Civil War, and a bloody one; it was nightfall, and the main action had moved on into the distance, leaving a blighted landscape of the dead and dying. Through all of this staggered a young man in the uniform of the Union, no more than a teen-ager. His field coat was smoke-blackened and torn, his eyes too bleak for one so young. His name was Joshua Hawthorn and he'd been separated from his company.

To make a bad situation worse, a brush fire had taken hold. The two armies had met in dense woodland that frustrated any cavalry charge and offered no direct targets for cannon. The lines of command had been broken, and there was chaos. Now, as the light faded, the underbrush was ablaze. Smoke drifted across the churned-up ground wherever there was a clearing, and artillery fire continued to fall at random.

Joshua scrambled over the lip of a crater and down the other side, almost landing on a cavalryman who lay pinned by his slaughtered horse.

'Sir!' Joshua gasped. 'I've lost my company! Which way to the line?'

It took him a moment to realise the obvious; that although the man's eyes were open the rider was dead, frozen in a position of struggling out from under.

Joshua moved on. He was lost, disorientated; he was trying to find his way back, but it was almost hopeless. When he broke into the next clearing, battlefield scav-engers rose from looting a corpse and scattered as the boy came into view.

He paid them no attention. Scavengers were no hazard; they were cowards who always fled from the living. More disturbing were the stories of ghosts on the battlefield, the shadows of men who lay dead, yet could be seen wandering hours later.

The scavengers had been stripping a Union soldier. One had been trying to prise the sword from the officer's hand; it was a ceremonial weapon with a decorated blade, of some apparent value. The hand and blade dropped to the ground, and Joshua thought he saw life in their movement.

He fell to his knees by the body. When he lifted its head from the mud he recognised the face of his commanding officer.

'What of my legs?' the man gasped. 'Those ghouls took my boots and I felt nothing.'

'I see your legs, sir,' Joshua told him. 'Your boots are gone but the rest of you is whole.'

'Good,' he said. 'Don't let them have my sword.'

Those were his last words.

Joshua looked all around and called out, 'Help for the captain!' But the only response was the moans of the dying, from all directions in the advancing night.

He closed the officer's eyes, as he'd seen the surgeons do. There was nothing else he could offer. With care, and meeting no resistance now, he took the sword from the dead man's fingers.

Then, weaponless no more, he scrambled onward.

Another clearing. Every clearing had become a scene of battle at some point in the day. Making his way forward, Joshua clambered over the wreck of a mortar. It had been dug in behind an abutment which had collapsed, tipping over the heavy weapon and crushing at least one man beneath it.

From this raised vantage point, Joshua desperately scanned the scene before him. Explosions continued to light up the sky, despite the hazard of mortar rounds falling on friend and foe alike.

One sound from the sky began to drown out all others. It was the rising shriek of an incoming shell, approaching fast. Joshua leapt from the abutment and started to run. Within seconds the mound was hit, the unburned powder in the mortar ignited, and night turned to day as he made it to cover just in time.

In the safety of a shell hole, he protected his head as the dirt rained down. It pelted him for a few seconds and then it stopped. When he started to look up, a hand grabbed his arm and he almost cried out in shock. He was not alone in the crater.

It was a sergeant of the artillery company, badly wounded and blinded, his eyes covered with a filthy bandage. He felt the sword in the young man's hand and assumed that he was talking to an officer.

'Captain!' he said. 'They lied to us. About the enemy. It's not the Greybacks. They're not even h—'

Another, even closer explosion cut him off. When the smoke cleared and Joshua raised his head, the sergeant too was dead.

After a few seconds, Joshua pulled himself free of

the dead man's grasp and crawled out of the shell hole. All around him was blazing white as if seen by the light of a thousand flares; and, in this unreal illumination, he witnessed something that he could hardly believe.

'Holy Mary, mother of . . .'

Spoken under his breath, the words faltered and then failed him.

Before him were enemy soldiers. Three of them. But they were an enemy unlike any that he'd ever seen in his short career.

Pale and vicious-looking, they wore rags under hastily donned uniform jackets that they'd taken from corpses and thrown around their shoulders. Rags of uniforms of different armies, some that he couldn't recognise. These were not the usual battlefield scavengers, stripping corpses of their clothes and possessions.

They were rotting cadavers, and they were raising the fallen dead.

They'd found a corpse and were checking it. On finding it more or less intact, one took the body's face and kissed its forehead.

After a few moments the body began to twitch and stir.

One of the creatures was Joshua's commanding officer; the limbs that had failed him in life had found new strength in death. Eyes that were clouded had begun to see again. The raised ghoul turned its face in Joshua's direction. When it spotted the sword, it flew at him with frightening speed.

There was no opportunity to run. The fight was short and brutal. The boy was outclassed but, when the ghoul was momentarily distracted by a bugle sounding a retreat nearby, Joshua saw his chance and plunged in the sword, almost to the hilt.

The creature looked down. It appeared to feel no pain. Then it looked to where its fellows were leaving the clearing, taking with them the dead that they'd raised.

Out of the smoke rode a cavalry officer, and when he saw the scene, he spurred his horse towards them.

The creature pulled itself off the blade and ran after the others.

Joshua was left, sword in hand, disbelieving and panting.

The cavalry officer reined in his horse alongside him, and shouted words of encouragement from the saddle.

'Congratulations, young man,' he roared. 'Your first kill? Don't stop now. We have them on the run!'

Joshua recognised him, from an earlier action at Tranter's Creek. In civilian life he was a college professor. Now he was a classical scholar with a horse and a gun.

Joshua called out, 'What are we fighting, sir?'

'Monsters, boy,' the man cried out. 'Monsters! And one of them's wearing the Kairos Ring!'

With that, he spurred his horse onward into the smoke, and the boy, all fired-up with the infectious fever of battle, followed with sword in hand, looking for a new enemy to fight. This, despite the fact that his first creature kill was hardly a kill at all, given that it hadn't stayed dead.

He could hear more of the horse soldiers behind him, crashing through the woods on their mounts. Could it be true? Had the course of the battle turned? Within a hundred yards or so, he saw a shape in the fog and gave chase. He followed the figure and found himself emerging from the woods into an open field where command tents and wagons stood.

It was the enemy's base camp. Joshua's brio evaporated and he stopped abruptly. There were too many here to fight, and none of them Greybacks; the monsters had taken the camp, and the dead they'd raised stood in a patient horde. He dived for the nearest cover, among the stacked barrels of an ammunition dump.

The monsters had a leader, it seemed, distinguished from the others by a golden breastplate and a crown of dead laurel leaves. Joshua saw him draw off a gauntlet to reveal a bony claw sporting a golden ring; this, at a guess, was the so-called Kairos Ring. The leader flipped open a split cover to reveal a chip of something that sparkled more fiercely than any jewel and then, making a fist, used it to inscribe an oval in the air.

The ring seemed to cut the air like a diamond on a window. It made – impossibly – a hole, a hole out of nothing, suspended in the air like a lion-tamer's hoop.

By the sounds they made, the horse soldiers were almost here. The ghoulish leader picked up a burning branch, holding it like a torch to light the way, and stepped aside. He grabbed the shoulder of the nearest corpse and the first of the dead was thrust into the shimmering aperture, stumbling through and disappearing.

The others picked up the idea and began to follow.

Joshua watched as the rest were sped on their way, vanishing from the scene like volunteers in some impossible stage illusion until only the leader remained.

Now the creature turned, scanning the clearing, and raised the burning brand above its shoulder. Almost too late, Joshua realised its intention. One hard throw and the torch spun high in the air towards the powder kegs, trailing fire and smoke. Joshua broke cover and began to run.

He did not mean to enter the hole in space. But the explosion sent him through.

Joshua hit the floor, hard. A stone floor. The captain's sword clattered on the ground beside him.

He was deafened and dazzled by the powder blast that had carried him over, but otherwise he seemed largely unharmed. He rolled over and looked back, expecting to see a reverse window onto the battlefield.

But all he could see was a big old mirror hanging on a bare stone wall.

It was oval and mounted in a gilded frame. The frame was ornate, dusty and strung with cobwebs. He saw himself reflected there, lying on the floor of a castle corridor. Beside him lay the broken-up dust and bones of the creatures' leader.

Joshua looked down. The dry corpse had not been robust enough to endure its chosen exit. Amidst the debris of its passing, the Kairos Ring shone gold.

Carefully, and fighting his revulsion, Joshua picked the ring out of the dirt. After all, he might be far from home, and a traveller like him couldn't afford to pass up such a gift of portable treasure. He blew off the dust; it swirled in the air, poured down in a stream, and reattached itself to the bones on the floor.

Joshua scrambled to his feet. The creature was reassembling.

He stared for a moment, to be sure that his eyes weren't deceiving him.

They were not.

He picked up his sword and slid the ring onto his finger as he moved away. His instinct was to run, but caution slowed him. He didn't know this place. It was like nowhere he could recognise, and a corpse army had preceded him. It was the very definition of dangerous ground.

This corridor led to another, and then to a junction,

which brought him to an empty hall. Each space that he passed through seemed to bear the mark of a different time, a different builder. He'd yet to see a window, but he thought he sensed a breeze and followed it. In one place, the scent of perfume; in another, that of some animal he couldn't identify. He saw no life, just desertion. Here, a bridge over darkness. There, an empty garden with a red sky.

And, finally, voices.

They echoed from deep in the shadows of a vaulted cellar. The walls were of brick and the shadows were thrown from lamps that must have been tended by some unseen hand. He could hear a woman speak, and – was that a man? It was so deep, and the tone of it raised the hairs on the back of Joshua's neck.

The woman was saying, 'When they want to move, they can really move.'

And the other: 'They're using the ring again.'

The woman said, 'Do you know what it is?'

And the other again: 'My best guess? The crystal form of dwarf star alloy. It's their key to the Gateway. It will cut through space and time like a diamond through glass.'

'That should make it impossibly dense,' the woman said. 'How can it not be?'

Came the reply, 'A secret known only to the Ancients.'

The woman said, 'We still don't know what the Sluagh want.'

The Sluagh? Was that what the dead things were

called? The name triggered a resonance in Joshua's memory, bringing with it an unexpected echo of his Irish grandmother's voice.

While thinking this, he almost missed hearing the woman say, 'Perhaps the boy listening from the shadows can enlighten us.'

Joshua froze.

'Come out,' the woman called.

Dare he? Perhaps he should. They didn't sound hostile.

From his hiding place, Joshua inched into the open. He saw the woman. She did not seem unfriendly. The other speaker was partly hidden in the shadows behind her.

'I have a sword,' Joshua warned her.

'You won't need it,' she said. 'We're not your enemies.' And then her attention was caught by the gleam of the Kairos Ring. 'Is that—?' she began, but didn't get to finish because the figure behind her had also seen the glint, and now he stepped forward into the light.

'How did you get the ring?' demanded the great golden beast, and Joshua dived in terror for the nearest doorway.

He heard the woman calling after him, but he paid her no heed.

This was a castle of nightmares. He ran and kept on running, as fearful of what lay behind him as of anything that might lie ahead.

Again, he sensed a breeze. But it was a wind with a bitter edge, of a kind he didn't know. He followed it anyway. By a shattered mirror, across a hallway littered with the armour of fallen warriors, and out onto a terrace beneath a dark fog of a sky. These were gardens, strangely crystalline. But the farm boy's reserves of wonder were exhausted now.

At the far edge of the terrace was a low stone parapet. Joshua reached it and looked over. Had he found the end of this place? Could this be a way back to the world he knew?

The wall below the parapet stretched down. And down. And down. There was no end to it. Just a descent into a bottomless void.

Disappointed, he turned back. Only to find that the army of the dead, the Sluagh, had silently assembled on the terrace behind him.

Before them stood their leader, resplendent in his breastplate and laurel crown, now fully reassembled from the dust into which he'd fallen.

These were the dead who could not die.

Although, as Joshua now discovered, they could speak.

Their leader pointed an accusing finger. The dead throat made a sound like cracking bones while in Joshua's head, like a whisper in a dream, the word formed: 'Thief.'

Joshua replied with spirit. 'Better a thief than a ghoul.'

'Return what you stole.'

'This?' Joshua held up the hand with the Kairos Ring for all to see and flipped the cover to reveal its glow. There was a gasp when he stretched his hand out over the void. The ring was loose on his finger; it might easily fall.

The Sluagh leader said, 'Let us bargain. Tell us what you want.'

'I'd rather die.'

'Then die.'

The horde behind the leader began making a strange noise. Joshua realised that they were laughing. They started to move towards him in a mass. He looked down. The drop went on for ever.

Joshua took a last glance at the approaching creatures, and then turned again to the void.

Was he brave as he faced his fear, or was he simply weary of being afraid?

'God save the Union,' he shouted, and jumped.

He heard screams, or screams of a kind, but they rapidly receded.

Joshua tumbled over and over. The Kairos Ring cut a spiral through space as he fell.

His landing was nothing like what he might have expected.

It was a soft landing. In fact, it was on a bed. A bed with a floral cover and, on display all around it, various matching accessories.

Later, and in a quieter moment, he'd be told that he'd landed in the soft furnishings section of a large department store in twenty-first-century London. The abrupt arrival of this soot-stained, battle-tossed youth with his wild eyes and brutal-looking sword triggered a commotion among the Christmas shoppers.

Instantly defensive, Joshua leaped to his feet on the bed, sword at the ready and breathlessly looking all around for any attack.

What kind of place was this? A fake bedroom with only two walls, fully made up and open to the world, one of many such displays through which oddly dressed people were now screaming and fleeing in alarm at his arrival. Joshua hopped down from the bed and staggered a little as he adjusted to the solid floor. There were bumps and crashes, as lamps and furniture fell over.

The crowd surged and changed direction like a shoal of fish as he crossed the floor. Joshua could see no clear way out. But as the people fled he could see men in uniform coming his way. Some had devices they spoke into as they moved.

'Come on, son,' he heard one of the men call to him. 'It's not worth it.'

By now he'd worked it out; this place was like a Dime Store, but on some bizarre and enormous scale. Next to the fake bedrooms stretched an acre of plates, pots, and pans. Beyond these he could see racks of clothing.

And now he saw a door marked Changing Rooms. He made for the door, only to find his way blocked by one of the uniformed guards.

The man certainly didn't lack nerve. He'd picked up a pillow as defence against the blade. It was a sound idea, but one which Joshua countered with a blow to the head from the sword's hilt. The unarmed man went down, and Joshua felt bad.

But he was through the door. He slammed it behind him, put his back to it to keep his pursuers out, and looked around.

He was in a short passageway with a line of cubicles down one side. Each cubicle had a curtain. In some there were clothes on the floor, hastily abandoned.

There was no way out.

Through the door he heard a voice calling out in an attempt to calm the situation. 'No one has to worry. We've shut him in, and the police are on their way. He's a very confused lad.'

And another voice, almost certainly the man he'd struck: 'Confused lad? He nearly broke my nose.'

So this was it. The place for his final stand. He'd survived a war, escaped from ghouls, evaded a monster, thrown himself into the void and lived. But in the end, it came to this. Now they were coming for him.

He slipped the Kairos Ring into his pocket, the better to take a two-handed grip on his late captain's sword. Somewhere far off he could hear a howling, a banshee siren of a sound. And then a banging. They'd started breaking in the door to reach him.

Joshua Hawthorn, nineteen years old, faced the door, backed off to the end of the short passageway, and for the second time that day prepared to die.

A foot burst through just before him. Not through the door, but through this flimsy inside wall of plaster and board. A couple more kicks and the wall split, and then the woman broke through in a cloud of white dust.

She stood before him and seemed to feel no threat from him or his blade. She spat dust, fanned the air a couple of times, and said, 'I wouldn't stay here if I were you.'

He recognised her from the vaulted cellar. He said, 'Who are you?'

'I'm not one of the Sluagh, that's for sure,' she said. 'My name is Romana.'

'The Slu . . . ?'

'Explanations later,' she said. 'Come with me.'

Romana was thinking that Joshua showed impressive resilience, given what he'd been through over the past few hours. When he hesitated to go with her, she said, 'It's all right. We're on the same side.' And without waiting she turned and stepped back through the rip in the wall.

A moment later, she heard him follow.

'You're not with the Union,' he called from behind.

'Same side, different war,' she said.

These were the back ways of the department store, in corridors that were narrow and less well-lit. She led the boy down two flights of stairs and into a loading bay, where she had a black cab waiting.

Now to see what he made of London. The city of his arrival stood more than 150 years in his future. She pushed him into the taxi.

'Ain't no horses,' he protested.

'Just horsepower,' she said, closing the door. And then, to the vehicle, 'Back to base.'

'Affirmative, mistress,' the driverless cab responded. The engine kicked in and they rolled out into the streets behind the store.

She looked at Joshua. 'Anything you want to ask?' she said.

'Those rotten body people,' Joshua said. 'You said you'd explain.'

'The Sluagh,' she said as they travelled. 'Also called the Souls of the Unforgiven Dead. They're using that ring to build an army in Hell. That's how Laszlo describes it, but sometimes Laszlo can get a little too poetic. They *are* following a plan; we just don't know what it is. Where's the ring now?'

She could see that he was only half-listening, transfixed by the startling new world outside the vehicle.

'I lost it,' he said absently.

She could see he was lying. 'That's a pity,' Romana said, and let it pass.

They'd reached Trafalgar Square. Joshua was staring out through the cab's tinted windows at the stone lions at the foot of Nelson's Column.

He said, 'Is Laszlo the name of the monster?'

'Monster?' she said, and then caught on. 'Oh. That's funny. I'll have to tell him. But yes. I suppose he is. When we're in town he doesn't like to go out. You can't easily disguise a Tharil.' Then she raised her voice and said, 'Take Gower after Oxford Street. It's faster.'

'Gower Street, affirmative, mistress,' the cab replied. Joshua hardly noticed. He'd already accepted a carriage with no horses; a carriage that spoke wouldn't be much of a leap.

When they reached their destination, a door rolled up to receive them and they entered another loading bay much like the last. Joshua was still clutching his sword when he climbed out of the cab.

His first ever journey in a passenger lift made him start as they began to descend. To distract him, Romana said, 'Don't worry about Laszlo, he's not as fearsome as he looks. Though he can switch it up if he needs to.'

'Pardon me if it's rude to ask,' Joshua said, 'but what is he?'

'I told you, he's a Tharil. Very ancient race. They have a special relationship with the fabric of time. Did they teach the Many Worlds Interpretation at your school?'

'Miss Fisher taught us to read . . .' he began.

She said, 'A Tharil can read the many paths a single moment can take and ride the time winds across them. That last place you escaped from? It's a gateway. *The* Gateway. The Tharils created it to expand their range through all of time and space. And those ... rotten body people, as you call them, the Sluagh, they've infested it for their own purpose.'

'Their purpose being what?'

'That's what all of this is has been created to find out,' Romana said, and the lift door opened.

They moved out, and onto a gallery.

Below them was an enormous subterranean hall. There were reading tables, at least a hundred of them, each with its own working light, most with a figure working on some different piece of material. They were handling huge books, bound volumes. And scrolls, papyri, stone tablets, waxed wood fragments ... every form of writing and record keeping through the ages was represented here, each item getting its separate scrutiny.

Romana said, 'We're underneath the British Library. It's a secret facility and these are all volunteers. Experts in so many fields and recruited throughout the ages to address this one challenge. You're not the only long-distance traveller here, Joshua Hawthorn.'

She explained how this organisation had been created in response to the Sluagh threat. This army of volunteers was combing ancient accounts and manuscripts for references to their appearance throughout history. For millennia, the Sluagh were thought to be a horde of minor preternatural creatures, somehow drawing their life-energy from the souls of battlefield dead; but at some point something happened that made them organised, more dangerous, their numbers increasing exponentially as they began working towards some unknown purpose.

'So, there you are, Joshua,' she said. 'It may not be the service you signed up for, but you're in a different army now.'

'Those are real scholars,' he said. 'My schoolhouse was eight kids in one room and we stopped all our lessons for the planting season. What do you think I can do for you?'

'You said you can read.'

'Not that well.'

'We'll find you something. Sometimes experience counts for more than learning. We'd no reader of Ancient Sumerian, so Laszlo jumped me back 5,000 years to recruit some Ancient Sumerians.'

She cast an eye over Joshua. He was a scrawny youth. She reckoned that he probably hadn't eaten in some time, and then only field rations, so she said, 'Come with me,' and led him to their dining hall. Like everything else in this secret facility, it occupied space that was separated from the public areas of the library. As they moved along, she noticed that he stuck the military sword through his belt and left it there.

As they walked, she said, 'By the way. You might hear that the Tharils were kings once. Don't mention that around Laszlo. You'll never hear the end of it.'

There were a few people in the dining hall, which also served as a break room and social area. She watched to see how Joshua would react to the sight of aliens among the human faces, but now he took them in his stride. Many of those who worked on the Sluagh project were survivors of massacres on other worlds, rescued and brought here through time and space.

They stopped beside a young woman at one of the tables. She wore a red robe with a simple headband.

Romana said, 'This is Nisaba. One of our Sumerians. Nisaba, this is Joshua.'

Nisaba smiled pleasantly and said, 'Is he coming to work here?'

'You might say he's fallen in with us,' Romana said. 'Are you hungry, Joshua?'

And Nisaba said, 'Join us.'

'I've no appetite,' Joshua said. 'Maybe later.'

They went to find Laszlo. He was standing in a darker part of the book gallery, watching the activity in the bright area beneath.

As they approached the Tharil, Joshua said in a low voice, 'I have a confession.'

Romana said, 'You do?'

'I didn't really lose the ring.'

'I knew that,' she said.

'I'm sorry,' he said. 'I just wasn't sure who I could trust.'

'Fair point. How do you feel about that now?'

By way of an answer, he dug around in his pocket, looked alarmed for a moment when he didn't find the ring straight away, then produced it.

'Laszlo?' said Romana, 'You see this?'

Laszlo turned. Joshua held out his hand with the ring lying flat on his palm for them to see. It had a finely wrought gold mount, with a hinged cover like a reptile's closed eye. Laszlo reached out and took the jewel. With enormous care he opened the cover to expose the tiny sliver of crystal at the centre of the mount. It was so thin that it could only be seen side-on; when turned to its edge, it vanished.

Joshua said, 'I think it's called the Kairos Ring.'

They both looked at him.

Romana said, 'How would you know that?'

'One of our officers. He was a college professor back east. All about the Romans and such.'

Laszlo returned his gaze to the jewelled piece. 'The Kairos Ring. Our first solid piece of information.'

'We can pursue this,' Romana agreed, and then she looked at Joshua. 'See?' she said. 'You've made a contribution already.'

*

No one could tell him how long he'd have to stay, but Joshua didn't complain. War had taught him to live in the moment. As a soldier he'd been told where to go, when to stop, who to fight, where to sleep. Here they gave him a pleasant little study cubicle to bunk down in and let him plan his own day.

In his low moments he felt some unease. Might his fellows call him a deserter? But he wasn't here by choice. And the fight went on and he'd already made a difference, which was more than he'd achieved in two years of soldiering.

He was introduced to others. They included the Librarian, a man of uncertain antiquity who radiated kindness and intelligence. The Librarian gave him a small charm to wear round his neck. He called it a Language Monitor and said it would help Joshua to converse with any stranger he met. He also assigned Joshua a reading table of his own. Within hours, a pile of books and bound newspapers had appeared on it.

Joshua was intimidated by the pile and avoided his table for quite some time. He took any opportunity to talk to Nisaba, the Sumerian girl who'd been his first introduction. He contrived to be around the dining hall whenever she took a break from deciphering the cuneiform script on the library's collection of tablets. The Sumerian writing consisted of wedge-shaped marks pressed into soft clay with a stylus; Joshua was awe-struck by the ease with which she read them.

One time she asked him, 'Do you miss your home?'

He gave a shrug. 'Don't you miss yours?' he said.

'I did for a while,' Nisaba said. 'Then I got used to shelter and safety. No one ever beats me, I don't freeze at night, I don't fear the dark and I'm no one's property to use as they please.'

'You were a slave?'

'They called us mountain girls. But that was just another name for it.'

'I'm fighting for the Union,' Joshua said. 'We're agin slavery.' He paused and considered for a moment. 'I think.'

'Laszlo will love you for that,' Nisaba said. 'His people were enslaved.'

In Joshua's mind this brought the two conflicts together. He saw a purpose in his presence, and began to apply himself to the research he'd been given.

All of the material on his desk was from the War of the Rebellion, but it was confusing. In some histories the Union prevailed, in others the South prevailed and a slave empire spread across the north. It made no sense until Nisaba explained to him that the materials were from different timelines. All futures were possible. None was inevitable.

He was embarrassed when the Librarian spotted him struggling with some of the harder text, following the words with his finger.

'I've something that may help,' the Librarian said. 'Wait there.'

He disappeared for a while and came back with a device.

'Put this over the text and press the button,' he said. Joshua did as instructed and the device began to read the words aloud.

'Best used with the earpiece if others around you are concentrating,' the Librarian said.

Joshua nodded. 'Then they won't know I'm stupid.'

'No one who engages with a book is any such thing.'

'How long have you worked here?'

'Since our doors opened,' the Librarian said. 'Before that I was with the King's Library. Overall, longer than you can imagine.'

It was at this point Joshua noticed, for the first time, that the Librarian's fingers were webbed and his nails were hooked, like claws.

The Librarian said, 'Anything you need to ask, you can come to me.'

'I do have a question.'

The Librarian waited, and Joshua said, 'Kairos. That's a word those old Romans used, right?'

'It's Greek.'

'Oh.'

'In rhetoric, *kairos* is, and I quote, "a passing instant when an opening appears which must be driven through with force if success is to be achieved".'

'Sounds like I really can ask you anything.'

'A good library can answer any question within

reason. For questions beyond reason, you need a librarian.'

Laszlo held the ring in his fist as he and Romana made their way into the library's archive storage. The Tharil had no need of the ring's time-cutting properties, but when holding it he could read something of its singular past and multiple futures. Its value couldn't be overestimated. It offered them a key to the movements and motives of the Sluagh.

The archive featured compact shelving that slid along rails; Romana cranked a handle to open a gap between the shelves, revealing an antique mirror at its far end.

From here they passed on through, and into the Gateway.

The signs of the Sluagh were everywhere. 'They trail their filth wherever they go,' Laszlo said in disgust.

'Focus, Laszlo,' Romana urged him.

'I *am* focused. This way.'

He continued to hold the ring in his fist. Like a music hall muscle reader, he allowed himself to be guided by the subconscious impulses that it triggered.

Romana memorised the journey as they moved. In some respects, the Gateway resembled a TARDIS, an apparently endless structure that needed more than three dimensions to map it. But while the TARDIS travelled, the Gateway did not. Situated on the border between E-Space and N-Space, it was a complex of chambers and gardens with infinite exits for those who know how to find them.

They reached a room with a stone portal. It had an artificial look, like a museum reconstruction. Romana touched Laszlo's arm and their phases shifted. They crossed the threshold to step out into darkness and firelight.

They were in a temple. They'd emerged, not through a mirror, but though a slab of polished obsidian at the base of a statue. On an impressive scale, and painted in colours, it portrayed a woman in robes and armour.

Laszlo looked up and said, 'One of their gods?'

'Athena,' Romana confirmed. 'War and wisdom.'

There was a crash. They caught a fleeting glimpse of a figure. He'd just dropped a plate and was running out of the temple into daylight at the far end. Romana followed, with Laszlo close behind.

They emerged into the sanctuary area before the temple. Here it was all blazing sun, white stone, and sand. At its centre stood an altar laden with fruit, gold, flagons of wine and expensive cloth.

'Tributes,' Romana said. 'A lot of tributes. Usually, it's just animals and food. These are people in trouble.'

'The Kairos Ring led us here. It must have significance.'

'We need to find out exactly where we are.'

Outside the sanctuary they were confronted by a

small crowd of people, who immediately threw themselves down onto the ground.

The nearest of them rose to his knees, covering his face with his cloak and calling out, 'All praise to Athena, and to the child of Typhon and Echidna!'

Laszlo said, 'To the child of what?'

'Typhon and Echidna,' Romana said. 'I think he means you.'

'So that makes you Athena? They think you're their goddess?'

'Go with it,' Romana said.

'Am I a god too?'

'Shush,' Romana said, and then called, 'Stand forward, priest of Athena.'

Head still covered by his cloak, the figure shuffled forward on his knees.

She said, 'Let the goddess see your face, and speak.'

'You heard her,' Laszlo growled. 'Show your face.'

There was a wail of terror from the crowd. The cloak dropped to reveal a scared boy.

Romana said, 'Don't fear. The gods are on your side. Speak.'

The boy spoke in a quavering voice. 'The ships came, and we surrendered to your will. The Spartans came, and again we bore our fate. But then came the Children of the Night.'

Laszlo said, 'What do you know of the Kairos Ring?'

The boy seemed confused. So, to get him back on

track, Romana said, 'Tell us about the Children of the Night.'

'They came after the battle to claim the wounded.'

'And?'

'They raised Critias and made him more powerful than ever. They follow him now. But in their eagerness to follow they left behind one of their own. And he's angry.'

'Show us,' Laszlo said.

The young priest led the way. Laszlo seemed to walk a little taller. He'd always been proud to be a king, now he was even happier to be a god. Romana hadn't the heart to tell him that the child of Typhon and Echidna was the Chimaera, lion-headed offspring of monsters. And female.

High on a promontory, looking across an inland bay where fires were burning, Romana could see a much bigger temple complex. By comparison, the one behind her was a mere shrine.

She recognised Athens, standing on its Acropolis. The Parthenon building was complete and the fires in the bay suggested a recent battle. That might help to fix on a date.

Romana returned her attention to more immediate matters. They were approaching a deep cistern lined with stone. There were four men around the opening, all holding long spears, all hovering nervously and looking down into the pit.

When she drew close, Romana could see that one of the Sluagh had been trapped down below. It was sloshing around in two or three feet of water and one leg wasn't working so well. Whenever it tried to leap and climb the wall, one of the men would jab with a spear and make it fall back.

Laszlo was right behind her, looking over her shoulder. 'I hope nobody plans on drinking from that,' he said.

The men around the pit froze at the sight of the gods. One dropped his spear and ran. The spear fell into the pit, where it landed with a splash.

The young priest said, 'What can we do if the dead won't die?'

'You could take the creature apart and burn the pieces,' Laszlo suggested. 'I'd like to see it come back from that.'

But Romana said, 'We need to take it back with us.'

'What do we want with a prisoner of war?'

'I want to find out what's driving them,' she said.

'As you wish,' Laszlo said. He handed her the Kairos Ring for safekeeping and stepped forward.

Everyone was yelling now because the Sluagh had picked up the fallen spear. The creature had braced it against the side of the pit and was trying to climb it like a pole.

Laszlo reached down, took hold of the spear, and raised it up with the Sluagh clinging on. As soon as it

212

came within reach, Laszlo grabbed its scrawny neck with his free hand. The creature would have been choking, had it had any need for breath. It flailed around and tried to reach Laszlo, but he held it at a safe distance.

'Let's get it back,' Romana said, 'before it shakes itself apart.'

They headed back towards the shrine, Laszlo with his arm held out straight and the choking, spitting Sluagh dangling above the ground.

'Run ahead of me,' Laszlo said. 'Prepare a cage.'

'I can't do that,' Romana said.

'You must.'

'I can't reach the Gateway on my own.'

'Romana,' Laszlo said, 'even a god's strength has its limits.'

His great arm was quivering. Romana could see the effort he was making to keep it steady. She had a sudden inspiration.

'There may be a way,' she said and set off across the sanctuary at a run.

'Praise Athena!' the people shouted after her. 'Athena, fleet as the wind!'

She entered the shrine, dodged the dropped plate and the spilled fruit offering left by the priest, and headed for the polished stone through which they'd arrived. Before it she paused, flipped open the ring, and drew a circle in the air before the surface. An opening formed. She forced herself to confidence. She didn't dare hesitate, but jumped forward . . .

And passed through.

She was back in the Gateway, at the point where they'd left it. Now she had to recreate the way home. A small feat of memory for a true Gallifreyan, but even Time Lords could make mistakes.

There was her mirror. A moment of doubt as the ring touched the surface, but the mirror parted like a skin of mercury and she fell out into the archives.

From there she ran to the main floor. Laszlo would be close behind.

'Librarian!' she called, and when he appeared, along with a number of curious scholars, she quickly explained what she needed. The Librarian picked out a couple of the volunteers and headed away.

Joshua was among those remaining. 'What can we do?' he said.

'Grab anything that looks like a weapon and come with me,' Romana said.

Joshua ran to his cubicle to get his sword, while the scholars mostly milled around and panicked. They met in the archives with an assortment of unlikely weapons that included kitchenware, umbrellas and a staple gun.

'They'll be coming through the mirror,' Romana said. 'Form a ring.'

At that point the Librarian and his volunteers arrived, all pushing a heavy glass display case.

Romana looked doubtful. 'Will that hold it?' she said.

'It'll hold anything,' the Librarian said. 'Five minutes ago, it was protecting the Magna Carta.'

They opened up the front of the case, positioned it facing the mirror, and formed a second line of defence behind it.

They were only just in time. The mirror shimmered and the Sluagh came through, still held aloft in Laszlo's grasp; but the Tharil's strength was all but gone, and this final effort wrecked him.

He dropped to his knees and the Sluagh escaped his grip. When its dead eyes saw the Kairos Ring on Romana's hand, it flew at her in sudden fury.

She stood her ground and saw the creature slam against the anti-bandit glass only inches away. It had failed to see the case standing between them. As soon as it was inside, Joshua jumped out and slammed the case front closed.

The Sluagh whirled about as Joshua panicked and fumbled the catch ... and then it stopped dead still, staring at him with its blank orbs.

Joshua couldn't help it. He shivered.

One of the scholars said, 'What do we feed it?'

Romana was moving to help Laszlo to his feet. She looked back over her shoulder and said, 'The story is that they eat human souls.'

The scholar looked blank and swallowed hard.

'They don't eat human souls,' she assured him.

Laszlo reached to accept her help, then remembered his dignity as a god and evaded her touch.

The captive battered against its prison for a while and then slumped into a corner of the case.

Romana said, 'The ring led us to a spot just outside Athens in the Hellenistic era. We were above the harbour, so I'd say we were in or close to the naval base at Piraeus.'

'I saw boat sheds burning,' Laszlo said.

'The citizens talked about a recent battle. Most of the buildings on the Acropolis were more or less complete so no earlier than around 330 BC, which rules out the Peloponnesian Wars. And a name was mentioned. Critias.'

The Librarian spoke up. 'Critias? A writer and philosopher. Pupil of Socrates.'

'Somehow all of this is tied together through the Kairos Ring,' Romana said. 'The question is, how? We've a time, we've a place, and we've a name. Let's focus the search.'

The scholars and volunteers dispersed, and Romana moved to look at the Sluagh. It shifted a little, so that it could see around her to Joshua.

Joshua said, 'That mark. On its forehead, there. Do you know what it is?'

Romana said, 'Why?'

'You know when you go to an open-casket funeral and they make you kiss your dead grandma goodbye?'

'No, but go on.'

'I saw one of these things do it to another and bring it to life. In exactly that place where the mark is.'

Romana took a closer interest in the mark, and the creature shifted, unhappily.

She said, 'You may have missed out on a formal education, Joshua. But never doubt that you're an asset.'

With those words in his mind and a glow in his heart Joshua wandered down to the study floor. He stopped by Nisaba's table, where she was organising a series of clay tablets into some kind of narrative order.

She broke off to take his hand and drew it under the working light to show how pale it was.

'When did you last go outside?' she said.

'I saw enough of outside to last me a long time,' Joshua said. 'Anyway, when did you?'

'I take myself up onto the roof sometimes. Everyone needs light and air. You should come with me.'

'Maybe I will,' Joshua said.

'If you don't look after yourself, you're going to fade away. Look how pale you are. Any more and we'll be able to see right through you.'

'Yes, ma'am,' he said. 'I promise you I'll do better.'

Then she shooed him away so that she could get on with her work. Others were at their own workstations, reading and researching. All around him the scholars were digging into Greek and Latin texts, while some of them looked into writings of the period in other territories and languages. Over on Joshua's table stood the Civil War histories and folders of photographs he'd been given. They were unlikely to have any relevance to a pupil of Socrates from an ancient land.

But no matter. He was an asset. That was official.

He thought about going to the dining hall, and got about halfway there, but decided he wasn't hungry. Back at his table, he tried reading for a while. Then he opened one of the folders and drew out an image that had been intriguing him. In it, three men stood by a tent in the woods. One was bearded and scarred. Some of the photographs had information written on the back, but this had none.

He slid the picture back into the folder as the Librarian passed by.

'Nisaba thinks she's found something,' the Librarian announced to everyone within earshot. 'You all might want to hear.'

They all met in one of the conference rooms and Joshua joined at the back. Nisaba was nervous at addressing a crowd, but Romana stood close to encourage her.

'I looked for any reference to Critias,' Nisaba said. She explained that she'd found a description of the Kairos Ring in a late Assyrian cuneiform text translating a lost Greek original. It told the story of the

Thirty Tyrants, a pro-Spartan government imposed on the Athenian people after the Peloponnesian War. Critias was their hard-right leader. He had been, as the Librarian had said, a writer and philosopher. His philosophy was to erase democracy through terror, executing his opponents and acquiring their wealth. The Kairos Ring had featured in a list of the treasures he'd seized.

She said, 'Critias had coveted the ring but he never dared test its power. He was killed when a group of exiles came back with an army to retake the city. It's not clear how, but he fell in the first battle. Now he leads the Unforgiven Dead just as he led the tyrants.'

'I've known men like Critias,' Romana said. 'Greedy, arrogant men who can never be wrong. If he's raising an army then I'll lay odds it's to go back and refight the battle he lost. He's not interested in the past, or in the future. He's out to get the place in history he wants, so he won't have to accept the one he actually deserves. Let's suppose his plan succeeds and he reinstates the rule of the Thirty Tyrants. Laszlo? What happens then?'

Laszlo, who'd been concentrating on one of Nisaba's clay tablets in his hands, looked up and said, 'I can see a line in which that could happen. It's not pretty to look at. Without the return of democracy, Earth's history becomes an endless dark age and with the Gateway at his service, Critias can spread the poison through all the known worlds. This is not what my Gateway was made for.'

Romana had a theory about the origins of the Sluagh, and now she had a subject on which to test it. With the help of a scanner borrowed from Imperial College and a contact in the pathology labs of University College Hospital, both of them just a stone's throw from the library, she was able to make rapid progress.

'It's a parasite,' she explained to her team just a few hours later. 'Interdimensional. So, it sits in the dead brain without taking up physical space, but the scanner could trace its effects in the right orbitofrontal cortex. They're neural circuits that light up with feelings of guilt, shame, and sadness. I've seen mind parasites before but never one this subtle.'

Laszlo said, 'And from there it drives the body?'

'Until the body's deteriorated too far to function, and then it moves to another by the process Joshua saw. Until then it's holding the host just this side of death.'

There was a silence as everyone took this in. The last traces of a living mind, used up in holding together a rotting frame. In such a state of perpetual torment, the Sluagh truly were the Unforgiven Dead.

Then Joshua spoke up and said, 'That kind of sounds like Hell.'

'A fair description,' Romana said, 'if you're the human

intelligence that it won't release. Critias is exceptional, and not in a good way. It's clear that he's never felt any guilt or shame. The parasite met its match in him.'

'And now the rest of them . . .' Joshua said. 'They're just another kind of slave.'

'Suffering to serve a master's glory,' Laszlo said.

'Would it help if we take down the master?'

'I'm working on it,' Romana said. She'd been thinking hard and could reach no easy solution. The simplest way to stop the parasite would be to destroy every host. At best it would equate to a mercy killing, but even that was something Romana couldn't countenance. And besides, it would be no easy business; as Joshua had witnessed, even the most broken Sluagh could reassemble itself and carry on.

Joshua said, 'I'm no general, but can I suggest a plan? Send me back into your Gateway with the ring. This Critias, he already knows I took it. He'll come find me and you can grab him.'

'Are you saying that you want to act as bait?'

'At Tranter's Creek we called it drawing fire. Look, I'll be fine. I know how this ends. I know I'll make it home. I've seen proof.'

Romana was about to speak but then Laszlo said, 'Do it,' and she offered no argument.

Joshua went off to get back into uniform.

'He should be told,' Romana said.

And Laszlo said, 'Tell him after. Why make this harder than it already is?'

With Joshua back in uniform, and once more in possession of the Kairos Ring, they went over the plan. The three of them would take the captive Sluagh back into the Gateway, where Laszlo would lead the search until there was some sign that the Sluagh army was close. At that point they'd contrive to let the captive escape. If all went as planned the creature would find its way back to the horde, and the horde would come looking for the ring. When Critias reached Joshua, Laszlo and Romana would step in. Laszlo would hold back the horde while Romana disabled their leader. She'd be carrying an improvised taser that she'd rigged from a flashlight and some paperclips. From close study of the brain scans, she knew where to strike.

And after the capture ... well, dealing with the undead tyrant would be a whole new challenge.

They pushed the glass cube back into the archives and repositioned it before the Gateway mirror. Their captive pressed himself against the glass, staring at Joshua and the Kairos Ring. He'd made several attempts to break out, with no success. It had been a useful test; they planned to use the same cube to imprison Critias after they'd brought him back.

Romana said, 'Everyone ready?'

Joshua nodded. Laszlo gave a growl.

They sprang open the glass case, and Laszlo dragged the prisoner towards the mirror with his arm outstretched, ready to pass them all through. His hand made contact and the mirror began to shimmer.

At this point, everything went wrong.

The Sluagh had been waiting on the other side.

Romana saw the mirror heave out like a silver bubble and then burst, spilling bodies into the narrow space between the shelves. The first ones fell, and those behind surged over them. Laszlo stood his ground but was powerless to prevent the flow. The Sluagh went round, they went under. Some grabbed his arms and hung on. The first to reach the glass case slammed into it; the next wave slammed into them, and the combined force shunted it back to become no obstacle.

Now they were out, and in the library. And they were still coming.

Some of the scholars tried to stand their ground and fight. Others wisely fled. The horde kept on coming and there, striding through the heart of them, came Critias the cadaverous, in his tyrant's crown and armour. Laszlo attempted to grab him as he passed, but the Sluagh weighed him down.

Joshua was swinging about him with his captain's sword, cutting down every enemy he could reach. Romana fought off one, and then another, and then four came at once and had her pinned.

She could see that Critias was heading straight for the boy. His followers had stopped the sword with their own bodies and carried Joshua back to hold him against the wall. As Critias drew close, she saw the boy flip open the cover of the Kairos Ring and try for a blow at the tyrant's head; a good move that would have ended the creature for sure, had several of the Sluagh not seized his arm and held it in mid-air.

Critias spoke: 'Why take only the ring, when I can take the boy?'

Romana called out a warning and saw Joshua struggle as the creature took hold of his face and raised its dead lips to the boy's forehead.

But then one of the Sluagh, the captive from the glass case, barked something that she didn't hear.

Critias turned his head. 'No?' He looked more deeply into Joshua's eyes. 'No!' he said, and then released the boy's face. He wrenched the ring from Joshua's hand instead.

Critias struggled to get it over his own knuckles and onto his bent finger. Then he used his free hand to help the other make a fist. The dwarf star chip was still exposed.

Romana deduced with horror that he was preparing Joshua's execution.

With the horror, came inspiration.

'Sluagh!' she cried out. 'Host of the Unforgiven Dead! What do you want most?'

All but a couple ignored her until she added, 'You can be free!'

Critias made a gesture of dismissal. Then he realised that the heads of all his followers were turning towards Romana.

She went on, 'You've all committed acts of war. Now it's your guilt and shame that keep you enslaved. Critias has never known shame, so he spreads misery without consequence. But hear this. Only the good can feel guilt. The torment you feel means that there is good in you. One truly redemptive act could release you all. I think you know what I mean by that.'

There was silence. Critias laughed his rasping laugh.

But he laughed alone.

He realised that his followers were now looking at him.

'Unforgiven Dead,' Romana pressed on. 'Do the right thing. Do it and then forgive yourselves.'

The Sluagh understood very little, but they understood this.

Critias saw what was coming and moved with more speed than Romana would have imagined; he quickly bent and with the Kairos ring inscribed a circle around himself, dropping through it and out of sight.

With a frightening howl, the horde dived after him. Much as they'd crammed through the mirror, they made a screaming whirlpool as they converged on the hole in space and were funnelled away.

Joshua was left to pick up his sword.

'I think we can leave them to take care of their own,' Romana said.

Joshua said, 'But he wouldn't take me. Why?'

After a pause, she asked him, 'Don't you know why?'

Joshua nodded. 'I think I might.'

She followed Joshua to his table, where he opened a folder and drew out an old picture. Three men before a military tent, in the woods. One of them bearded, with burn scars.

He said, 'Here's the proof. That's me.' And then he looked at her with both hope and doubt. 'It is me, isn't it?'

'It is, and it isn't.'

He hesitated, and Romana's hearts broke a little for him.

Then he said, 'Am I a ghost?'

It was as if he already knew, if not the entire truth, then something of it.

She said, 'The Joshua in the photograph survived the explosion. The Joshua projected through the portal was what we call a photon shadow. A detailed map of light. Not unlike a photographic print. A rare phenomenon.'

Joshua stretched out his hand over the picture, and Romana realised that the process was even more advanced than she'd thought. She could see through his hand to the faces beneath. Like Joshua, she'd heard those stories of ghosts on the battlefield; the shadows of men who lay dead yet could be seen wandering hours later.

Joshua said, 'I thought the Sluagh prisoner knew me. The way it looked at me. But I realise now, it just saw what I was.' His eyes met with Romana's. 'What happens now?'

'You have a home here,' she said.

'Until my light fades away,' Joshua said.

She could sense the turmoil he must be feeling. The signs had been there from the beginning; the lack of injury from the blast, the absence of appetite, the aversion to bright light.

Joshua looked at the picture again. He said, 'That man's long dead. But I'm right here. And I did make a contribution, did I not?'

'You did, Joshua,' Romana said. 'You certainly did.'

He nodded. And closed the folder. 'OK,' he said.

She left him with his thoughts. As she walked away, Nisaba was heading towards him. Their eyes met briefly. Romana gave the slightest nod.

For Romana and Laszlo, there would be further adventures. With the Sluagh driven from the Gateway, its function could be restored. Romana would continue to follow the path of righteous science and daring that had been set by the Doctor. Her Tharil friend would continue with her as both teacher and companion, haunted by his own history but beginning to understand the value of compassion.

Most moved on. The secret base beneath London was closed and the scholars and researchers dispersed. But not Joshua. The Librarian undertook to be responsible for his welfare, and for Joshua the British Library became home. Surrounded by so many books, he accepted Nisaba's offer to help with his reading skills.

In the days and months to come, they'd sometimes be glimpsed in the stacks.

The quiet woman, and her companion ghost.

THE LITTLE BOOK OF FATE

The brewers' wagon dropped him off mid-morning on Station Road, and a shopkeeper washing his windows offered directions to Low Green and the Whitsuntide fair. The Doctor wanted to know if there had been any big changes to the fair this year, anything new and strange or out of the ordinary, and the toy seller took the opportunity to unload his grievance onto a stranger. The Corporation had made a bad decision in moving the event to the outskirts of town, he complained. After coal strikes and the Great War, people around here had less money to spend. Visitor money made a difference. Those tradesmen who'd objected to stalls and booths on the streets outside their doors had effectively turned such business away. Meanwhile few locals had anything good to say about the crush and dust and stench of the new fair ground.

When he could get a word in, the Doctor thanked him and set off.

A couple of people went by, glancing at the Doctor's

attire. Lifted from a medic's locker in San Francisco after his last, fraught regeneration, the frock coat had grown shabby, the buttons dulled. Not such a dandy as he'd once seemed, he drew less attention now.

He'd left the TARDIS seven miles back in Whitehaven, in plain sight on a street corner where no one would think its presence remarkable. A travelling fair was, by definition, something of a moving target. He got his first sight of it as he reached the railway, after hearing the notes of a steam organ drifting up the street.

There it was. Like a prairie village in a bend of the estuary, a nexus of noise and smoke on low-lying scrubland. People were coming in from different parts of town; families, children, small gangs of youths. He joined them on the path towards the showground.

Already it was busy. Probably had been since seven in the morning, when shift-working miners would have been gathering around the boxing booth for the chance of knocking out a professional and picking up a sovereign.

The Doctor moved through the daytime crowd, alert for anything. The centrepiece of the fair was the Racing Horses, an enormous bright carousel and the source of the calliope music. In a ring around the carousel were gaming stalls of frame and canvas and beyond them the swingboats and a shooting gallery, all funnelling visitors in towards the portables, the booth shows.

No one paid the Doctor any attention. Theirs were

hard lives and they were hungry for wonder. He stood by O'Brien's Golden Dragons and looked around. It would be a help, the Doctor thought to himself, if he had a more specific idea of what he was looking for.

Between the ghost show and a tacky Hall of Mirrors, he wondered if he might be on to something.

The spieler was working hard and a crowd was gathering. The man wore a loud checked waistcoat and a battered trilby hat. In his hand, flourished like a baton, was a silver-topped cane. He stood on a platform before a two-wagon fronted show made magnificent by a glorious frontage of painted flats and canvas and there he declaimed, as loud and expansive as any Roman orator.

'This is not an exhibition for the faint of heart,' he shouted across the heads of the crowd. 'If your curiosity is merely idle, pass on by. Beyond this curtain lies the true experience of wonder for those who both seek and deserve it. Sights reserved only for those of the wit and humanity to appreciate the infinite variety of our Lord's creation.'

The Doctor wasn't listening.

On the great canvas wall behind the spieler were images of promised wonders, some achievable, some impossible. They cavorted about the curtained entrance as if swirling in the clouds, the Sistine imaginings of a fairground Michelangelo. Creatures of myth. Medical unfortunates. Nature's mistakes.

One image had drawn and now held his attention. One creature. One wonder.

Alongside it was the one promise in the showman's lexicon that always had to be honoured.

LIVE

'Oh, my,' the Doctor said aloud. 'Really?'

A mauve alert had brought him: the highest form of interstellar distress call, a scream across time, impossible for any decent being to ignore. Fired off in a distant galaxy, it had vanished before he reached it. Only for its unique signal to flare again, briefly, in this specific region of twentieth-century Earth.

The far north west of England, to be precise. Somewhere along the coast, to be less so.

Then it happened again. And again. As if someone was collecting far-off disasters and bringing them here.

Intrigued, never able to resist a call for help, and – to be honest – looking to break a long spell with no company, he'd made his best guess, picked a spot, and pointed the TARDIS to it.

He'd arrived and found ... nothing.

And there it had seemed his search might end, were it not for the chance glimpse of a handbill pasted to a wooden fence behind a Whitehaven public house. It was the dates of the previous year's travelling fair, still just about readable. An ordinary person might see nothing worth noticing, but the Doctor was no ordinary person.

He saw a pattern. He saw possibilities.

Close by stood a brewers' wagon with a dray horse munching noisy oats in a canvas nosebag. The pub's landlord and a drayman were rolling a last barrel down a ramp into the yard.

The Doctor indicated the poster and said, 'I expect a travelling fair in town can bring in good business.'

'Not bad,' the landlord replied. He'd no jacket and had rolled up his sleeves for the work, exposing forearms of chiselled oak. He was thickset, somewhere between fifty and sixty years old, with curly grey hair around a bald crown. He added, 'Are you one of them?'

'What,' the Doctor said, 'show people? No. Do I look like one of them?'

'Not for me to say.'

He seemed sanguine enough. The Doctor followed him into the yard and said, 'How long did you spend at sea?'

Not so sanguine now. More suspicious. 'How do you know about that?'

'I can't match those splendid tattoos, but I can tell you I'm a veteran of many a long voyage myself.'

The landlord signed the drayman's paper and handed it back along with his pencil. The drayman went off to tend to his horse and the landlord said, 'Thirty years in the Queen's Navy. Volunteered to go back for the war but the King wouldn't have me. I see you now. You'll be one of those science chaps, up from Greenwich.'

A naval astronomer? It was an astute conclusion,

and the Doctor didn't argue. The landlord began to move and, with a tilt of his head, he indicated for the Doctor to follow him inside.

The house was not yet open, its panelled interior empty and dim. The Doctor said, 'A long-serving sea dog will be no stranger to the night sky. Have you seen anything odd since the fair came?'

'Odd in what way?'

'Strange lights. Falling stars. Anything up there not staying in its rightful place.'

'The missus went for her fortune told and got some good news, if that counts. Rum or beer?' He'd moved behind the bar counter to where the tapped barrels and serving jugs were.

The Doctor said. 'What can you tell me about the show people? Do they play the same towns in the same order every season?'

'They do. They call it the Cumberland Run. I've let them winter some of their vans in the yard these last couple of years. They've paid well for it, too. To be honest, it's helped me through some hard times. What's your interest, there?'

'I'll tell you what,' the Doctor said, drawing a seat up to the bar. 'You uncork the rum and I'll explain.' In truth he had no intention of explaining, or of actually risking the after-effects of Navy-strength spirit. The alcohol, he could process. The hangover, not so much. He said, 'What about the people?'

'They mostly kept themselves apart. Just as well, really. You expect folk like that to be a bit odd, but . . .'

The Doctor leaned in. 'Yes?'

'Well there's freaks, and then there's *freaks*.'

'And so, gentlefolk of Workington, if you pass through that curtain I can promise you a sight you will never forget: a living monster, half man, half lion. Yes! He is alive and he moves. Who can put a price on such enlightenment? But it's yours here, it's yours today, it's yours for just one, single, shiny sixpence!'

A shiny sixpence. Something of a problem, for a being who carried no money.

Twenty minutes later he was back, after assuring the boxing booth's owner that no, his best fighter wasn't permanently damaged, that he'd take his prize money in small change, and that if the man balked at paying he'd let the miners know that the house champion fought in gloves that were only half the padded weight of the challengers', making his punches twice as brutal. The Doctor gave out most of the change to the grubbiest-looking children and kept sixpence back for the show.

After handing it in at the paybox, he joined those being ushered up the steps and across the platform. All crowded in through the curtain and found themselves in a narrow, darkened space through which they began to shuffle in line. Every few feet they'd pass a table or enclosure with another tragic 'wonder'; specimens of the unborn in formaldehyde jars, a three-legged cock-erel from Hamburg, the inevitable Feejee Mermaid, a painted life-sized cut-out of the World's Tallest Man. After the line had doubled back on itself a couple of times they emerged into a wide and windowless room at the back of the wagons. Walls and ceiling were painted black and a single electric light shone onto a shabby red curtain. Somewhere close outside could be heard the chug of a generator, supplying power.

The spieler had now rejoined them.

'The Man Beast of the Serengeti,' he said. 'Captured and brought to England by the great explorer Henry Morton Stanley himself. Half man, half lion. Prince of the jungle, or the product of some unholy coupling? You decide.' And with that he thrust his cane into the curtain and swept it back.

Behind the curtain, bars. And beyond the bars, straw. And in the corner a huddled and dejected figure, head bowed, face turned away, but with an unmistakable mane of gold.

The crowd stirred uncertainly. 'By all means move closer,' the spieler urged. 'Those bars are solid iron, cast from the plates of a sunken German warship and forged in a Great British foundry.'

And with that he thrust his cane and arm through the bars of the cage, poking at the creature and causing its head to snap up, which brought a gasp of surprise from the audience.

Not least from the Doctor.

A Tharil. An honest-to-God, actual Tharil.

'Don't be misled by this show of torpor,' the spieler said. 'He can move when he needs to.' And with that he leaned in further and poked the stick harder. The creature swatted it away. The spieler prodded again.

Then everything happened at once.

In the blink of an eye the imprisoned Tharil flew across the cage and slammed into the bars, making a grab for the spieler who neatly skipped back out of reach. Most people were screaming now. The Tharil seized the bars and wrenched them back and forth with a power that made the entire wagon shake under their feet. The spieler called out something that sounded like a warning, but no one could hear him.

Then a pin flew, or something broke; the cage door was flung wide open and there was nothing between the raging beast and the crowd.

At the same moment, double doors at the side of the wagon burst out into daylight. 'Save yourselves!' roared the spieler, and the Doctor was carried forward in a stampede of panicking bodies.

It was all over in a second. With the last person out, the side doors closed like a trap, hauled shut on a rope by the same gaff lad who'd opened them on cue.

It was a most effective finale. One or two continued in their distress but for the majority it was a moment of relief and hysteria and a sense of sixpence well spent. They dispersed with a buzz of excited chatter.

The Doctor made his way round to the front of the booth, where a *Back in 10 Minutes* sign had been set out on the platform. He stopped at the paybox where a grandmotherly woman of around seventy, in a ratty fur collar and a headscarf, was counting change.

He said, 'Madam, can I ask you, who owns the show?'

And the woman said, 'Get lost, son, don't mither.'

He needed another approach. A more amenable lad on the shooting gallery pointed him to a painted caravan. At the foot of its wooden steps was an awning over a table and two chairs. A board with elaborate script read, *I will look on the stars and look on thee, and read the page of thy destiny.*

He climbed the first step to reach and knock on the door. He called, 'Hello?'

Waiting for a reply, he looked at the table. On it lay a pack of playing cards and a fan of cheaply printed booklets.

'You wish a reading?'

The voice came from behind him, making him start with surprise. He turned. This was the Fortune Teller? She was younger than he'd expected. Much younger, but with the quiet self-possession of one much older. She wore a full skirt and a Romany waistcoat with a green scarf knotted at her throat. On her head, a black beret.

He said, 'I was looking for the owner.'

Ignoring that, she said, 'Understand this first. The law forbids divination for payment. Buy one of my books for a shilling and the reading is free.'

The Doctor saw that he would have to play along. He began to undo his grey cravat.

'I rather stupidly gave my cash away, but this is silk,' he said, and held it out. 'Worth rather more than you're asking.'

'Then I have to wonder what you expect in return.'

'There's a Tharil in the freak show and set of astral phenomena that follow this fair around. Please don't try to say you don't understand.'

Rather than reply, she accepted the scarf, folded it, and tucked it away. Then she said, 'Shall we see what the cards have to say?'

The Doctor sighed inwardly. 'If we must.'

They sat, and without waiting for instruction he picked up the deck with his left hand and gave it a one-handed Faro shuffle. At no point did he take his eyes off the young woman.

She said, 'You're very skilled for a sceptic, Mr . . .'

'Doctor,' he said. 'I'll have you know I once wowed Napoleon Bonaparte with a psychic reading based on no knowledge and no belief in psychic ability on my part, which I think you'll agree makes it all the more impressive.' He set the deck down and cut it once. 'But then I had a young friend who performed small miracles with the toss of a coin so trust me, my mind is always open. But right now I'm ...'

'Shh.' Having raised her finger to her lips, she picked up the deck and dealt three cards to represent the Doctor's past, present and future. She turned the first card, for the past.

'Ten of Diamonds, reversed,' she said. 'So, before this came a journey, anxiety. Leading you to ...' The second card, representing the present. 'Queen of Spades, a faithful friend. And in your future ...'

'With me it's usually the Ace of Spades and it's never good.'

She turned over the Ten of Hearts.

'Rebirth,' she said, and looked up into his eyes. 'Doctor.'

'Romana,' said the Doctor.

They caught up, after a fashion. He told her of Adric's sad but heroic end. She told him of their encounter with the Sluagh, the Host of the Unforgiven Dead, and of its impact upon Laszlo. Where some of the liberated Tharils struggled to deal with the loss of their ancestral empire, others – to the derision of those who still fancied themselves masters – now sought a path forward. Along the way she'd devised an answer to K-9's vulnerabilities in the form of an upgraded AI that enabled him to migrate into any sufficiently advanced hardware and use its resources. Right now he was running their beacon surveillance from a student's gaming console in 2029. She would keep the silk for a souvenir; she unknotted her own cheap cotton scarf and offered it as a keepsake in return. Neither had much to say about the other's latest regenerated form, but the Doctor said, 'It's the hair, isn't it? I cut it myself. Probably a mistake.'

Through a door behind the empty Tharil cage they walked out into the back camp where the show people had their enclave. Caravans in a circle, and a temporary fence to screen them. Here they all ate, slept, and relaxed away from public view.

There was little relaxation about the place today; more a sense of urgency among the humans and aliens moving back and forth. He saw at least three Tharils, one of them escorting an injured Foli to a medical tent. He recognised him as the creature from the earlier performance, now in a much different character.

'Laszlo recruited them,' Romana explained. 'So many Tharils have lost their taste for empire. Some needed a new purpose.'

'So you set up a rescue station.'

'There's a war out there.'

'There's always a war somewhere.'

'This one's spreading, and it's getting more intense. We've created a set of portals in the Hall of Mirrors. The Tharil volunteers bring in refugees and we disperse them to new worlds and homes. The carnival's a perfect disguise. We're always on the move and no one's surprised by strange creatures passing through.'

Strange creatures, indeed. One of the rescue workers was a young Silurian who could pass, in a sideshow, for an Alligator Boy. He was speaking to an Omu that could easily rebrand as a Human Skeleton.

Someone was approaching Romana. It was the spieler from the freak show. The man now spoke to Romana with the deference due to a commanding officer.

He said, 'Distress call from the Sepharial system. Five dead out of three families and the survivors needing rescue. Faustine has the coordinates.'

'And Laszlo?'

'Laszlo's hurt, but he went back out.'

'Typical.' Romana beckoned for the Doctor to follow. Like the Cabinet of Curiosities, the Hall of Mirrors had a back way in.

The front-facing half of the booth was the public attraction. This back half was the transit station. Accessing their Gateway through the mirrors and using it as a hub, the rescue team could make their way to any geotemporal location to secure the safety of refugees. Through one-way glass the townsfolk could be seen, blundering around and giggling in eerie silence. They were ghosts, oblivious to all that was taking place on this other side.

Two of the gaff lads stood ready to receive the

casualties of war. Except that they weren't really gaff lads, and one of them had gills. Like many of the volunteers, this one was a refugee himself. He was about to speak to Romana but the shimmering of a tall mirror in an ornate gilded frame took everyone's attention.

The surface split. Like a statue being raised from water Laszlo emerged sideways from the mirror, taking care with his burden to stay clear of the frame. With him came a whiff of war, the scent of stone and dust and burning flesh. Across his arms lay the body of an adult Grellan, blue skin all but drained of colour. Laszlo began to buckle and would have sunk to his knees had the gaff lads not stepped in and relieved him of his burden.

Romana led him to a chair and made him sit. His face and hands were scorched, much of the fur burned away.

He said, 'It's bad back there. I heard children. I have to—'

'Stay,' Romana said. 'Get some attention, we need you in good repair. Doctor, give me your hand.'

It took a moment for the Doctor to understand.

But only a moment.

He gripped Romana's outstretched hand and they moved to the mirror together.

The sky reminded him of the burning of Rome. The battle was being fought off-planet with no regard for the lands or the people below. Missiles streaked across the upper atmosphere, cutting though the fading trails of previous barrages.

Here on the ground, a wasteland. The city had been evacuated, but no evacuation is ever complete. They followed the cries of children.

'Riding the time winds,' the Doctor said. 'I'm impressed.'

'So you should be,' Romana said. 'It's hard work.'

Though she'd developed her skills, Romana couldn't match the natural powers of a Tharil. She could, however, follow the rift created by Laszlo. He'd blazed a trail through time and space that would eventually fade, but which for now offered a pathway.

Ahead of them was a Grellan child, vainly waving a flag of surrender at the sky. When he saw them, he dropped the flag and ran.

Perhaps the rumours were true. That the Time Lords could become as feared as any other race.

As they scrambled over rubble to follow him, Romana said, 'This is what it's like. For every ship and distress beacon you tracked to us, there are a hundred one-off rescues like this.'

They found three children cowering in the corner of a cellar. The rest of the cellar had been blown open to the sky.

The Doctor said, 'We're not here to harm you.'

'They'll need convincing,' Romana said. 'It's a forever

war and it's spreading through all space and time. No side is coming out of it well.' And to the children she said, 'I don't expect you to trust me. But trust me.'

One of the children said, 'Machine creatures took over the citadel. Everyone else ran but we couldn't. Then the bombs started coming.'

The Doctor told them, 'We'll get you out of this. No Sepharian left behind.'

The bombs were falling closer as they made their way back through the ruins. For Romana to pass everyone through the portal, they'd need to link hands. She used their two scarves to fasten the children to each other, and then she and the Doctor each took an end of the Grellan daisy chain.

'Everyone hold tight,' she said.

As they were about to leave, the Doctor looked back. Far across the city a thread of smoke was rising into the air. Every few seconds it was interrupted, then continued. A signal for help? Not everyone had access to a distress beacon.

'No Sepharian left behind,' he said.

'We can only do what we can,' Romana said.

'I'll come back in the TARDIS and pick up the rest.'

When the TARDIS returned, he landed it squarely in the middle of the back camp. People of the town would swear that they heard an elephant somewhere. This time he'd brought back eighteen refugees; hardly more than a drop in an ever-expanding ocean, but every life saved was a push back against evil.

The medical team moved in. The resettlement volunteers moved amongst them, making their lists. Laszlo, recovered now, was off on another mission. The damaged passenger shuttle that he was piloting out of the midst of a firefight would be rediscovered some decades later at the bottom of Siddick Pond, only to be dismantled and removed within days by a government agency without a name.

As they watched these latest arrivals slowly grasping the idea that they were safe, Romana said, 'You could stay. Join us.'

'You're organised,' the Doctor said. 'You don't need me. But you can't be everywhere. I'll find wherever I can do most good.'

She nodded. It was much the answer that she'd expected.

'You didn't take your book,' she said, and produced one of the printed pamphlets taken from the Fortune Teller's table. 'You have to have it. It's the law.' She tucked it into his pocket, and adjusted the knot on his new green scarf.

'Thank you,' the Doctor said.

'Travel well,' she said.

In these darkening times, he promised he would try.

*

Later, when he was on his way, he remembered her gift in his pocket and took it out. He saw that it was the *Oraculum*, Napoleon's Book of Fate, a poor-quality English reprint of the volume that the superstitious emperor had supposedly carried with him throughout his campaigns. The book was a fake, of course, the work of a Grub Street hack, though the superstition was real. But as he'd tried to warn the man – if you rely on luck, what you get is Waterloo.

Quite a thoughtful gift, considering. He could feel that there was something in its pages. A solitary playing card. She must have slipped it in. He turned it face-up: it was the King of Diamonds.

The King of Diamonds. He thumbed through the flimsy pages to find its arcane meaning. The subjects there included moles, the weather, astrology, palmistry, physiognomy, Lucky Days, card divination . . .

'The King of Diamonds. A fair man of a fiery temper, generally in the army, but both cunning and dangerous.'

He had to smile.

How very apt.

How very Romana.